TAKE IT DOWN

BY
KIRA SINCLAIR

MILLS & BOON

First published in Great Britain 2012
by Mills & Boon, an imprint of Harlequin (UK) Limited,
Eton House, 18-24 Paradise Road, Richmond, Surrey TW9 1SR

© Kira Bazzel 2012

ISBN: 978 0 263 89732 6

30-0512

Harlequin (UK) policy is to use papers that are natural, renewable and recyclable products and made from wood grown in sustainable forests. The logging and manufacturing processes conform to the legal environmental regulations of the country of origin.

Printed and bound in Spain
by Blackprint CPI, Barcelona

When not working as an office manager for a project management firm or juggling plot lines, **Kira Sinclair** spends her time on a small farm in north Alabama with her wonderful husband, two amazing daughters and a menagerie of animals. It's amazing to see how this self-proclaimed city girl has (or has not, depending on who you ask) adapted to country life. Kira enjoys hearing from her readers at her website, www.kirasinclair.com. Or stop by writingplayground. blogspot.com and join in the fight to stop the acquisition of an alpaca.

I'd like to dedicate this book to three strong, savvy and supportive women—Vicki Lewis Thompson, Rhonda Nelson and Andrea Laurence. You guys are not only a font of information, but also a well of support that I'm so lucky to have in my life.
I couldn't do this without y'all!

Prologue

"WHY THE HELL ARE THESE people in my bedroom?"

Zane Edwards leaned back into a dark corner— the only spot in the place that wasn't buzzing with activity—and prepared for an excellent show. Between the photographer shouting instructions, his assistants moving furniture, light stands and anything else that got in their way, and Marcy constantly flipping through a clipboard of papers she hugged to her chest like a lifeline, the normally large space suddenly felt pretty small.

And Simon Reeves, his boss and longtime friend, was about to make it smaller.

Even from his melt-into-the-background location, Zane could see Marcy, the resort's manager, grind her teeth. Her skin paled before flushing an angry pink. Oh, goody, the fireworks were about to start. Up until now, his day had been pretty damn boring.

Marcy had asked him to shadow the production team there to take marketing and publicity photographs. Not exciting, although not much about his job as head of security for Escape, an adults-only Caribbean resort on Île du Coeur—an island just off the coast of St. Lucia—was.

He knew how important this shoot was to Marcy, though, so he'd do his part. She needed these photographs for a magazine ad campaign, and the deadline was fast approaching. They'd intended to feature a couple, but the pair they'd had an agreement with backed out at the last minute—after the photographs had already been taken.

The couple, Colt and Lena, had paid for the photographs and compensated the resort for the cost of production, so Escape wasn't out any money. But they'd definitely lost time. Marcy'd had to regroup and brainstorm an entirely new concept, since she didn't have time to hire more talent.

Apparently, Simon had forgotten he'd given Marcy permission to shoot in his private space. Not unusual when the man had his nose buried in that computer—which was always.

With a cutting tone of voice that reminded Zane of his high school calculus teacher, Marcy said, "This marketing campaign is going to bring us the kind of exposure that draws guests, Simon."

"We don't need more guests," was Simon's rather predictable response. It was entirely possible that Zane was the only person on the island who understood why the man had no desire to fill the resort to the rafters.

Fewer guests meant fewer disruptions, giving Simon the space and time he needed to write. Simon had his reasons for keeping his career as an author a secret—even from Marcy. Betrayal by someone you trusted could make you rather…reluctant to let people in. And Simon had definitely been betrayed. Courtney, his ex-girlfriend, had really done a number on him, stealing his work and passing it off as her own.

The only reason Zane knew the truth was because he and Simon had been friends since their fraternity days. They might have gone their separate ways after college, but they'd always had each other's backs. When Zane's life had imploded, Simon had been the first to offer him somewhere to stay, and when Zane had refused the handout, Simon had given him a job. Hence his position at Simon's resort.

Not everyone knew Simon had bought Île du Coeur not as a business investment but as a secluded place to come and lick his wounds. Apparently, the island was good for that. Marcy didn't know the truth, so she didn't understand. All she saw was a man who'd bought a resort and then didn't give a damn about actually making it run. Which was actually far from the truth. Zane knew Simon needed the place to support itself. The man had some money, but the upkeep for Escape was unbelievable and he needed to cover operating expenses.

"We have empty rooms, Simon. We need more guests. Especially during the off season."

Simon leaned languidly against the door frame, completely uncaring that every person in the room had stopped moving to turn and stare. "I like the off season just fine. I enjoy the peace and quiet."

Zane figured he had exactly thirty seconds to step in or Marcy was going to lose it. Her blue eyes flashed a warning that Zane knew Simon would ignore. A smile played at the corners of Simon's lips, almost as if he were looking forward to the fallout of whatever was going to come next.

And if there hadn't been an audience, Zane might

have slipped quietly out of the room and let it happen. The two of them had been striking enough sparks off each other lately to light the bonfire they held on the beach. But they weren't alone, so...

On silent feet, Zane moved between Marcy's glaring gaze and Simon's impish grin and said quietly, "Not the time or place, guys," tipping his head to the spectators.

Simon looked over Marcy's shoulder at the people staring, and his lips tightened into a straight line. Oh, that was worse. Marcy pissed he could handle. Simon angry was unusual and therefore infinitely more volatile. Even though Zane was an ex-CIA agent trained in fifty ways to kill with household objects, he tried to avoid Simon when the man's temper flared.

Simon's eyes narrowed as he looked around Zane to Marcy. "I don't want strangers in my space. I need to work."

Marcy snorted. Probably not the smartest thing she'd ever done. Zane widened his stance and braced for the consequences.

"Well, you're going to have to wait. The marketing director for the campaign specifically asked to photograph your private rooms, Simon. And you agreed."

"I did?"

"Yes. You're on the highest floor, with the best view. From this vantage point, we can show a luxurious room with the jungle behind surrounded by deep blue water."

It was uncomfortable, being at the center of their angry standoff. They stared at each other, through him, but Zane figured this way at least he wouldn't have to witness a murder.

"You're not going to go away until I let them do this, are you?" Simon finally asked.

"Nope," Marcy responded.

"Fine," Simon said, whirling around on his heels and heading for the door. "But I start throwing people out the window if you're not done in an hour."

Most people might think Simon was kidding. It was hard to take a man who dressed like a surfer seriously. But Zane knew firsthand that surf-god exterior hid a spine of steel and a drive to succeed. Hell, even he forgot sometimes. It was easy when Simon smiled that crooked grin.

With a huff, Marcy prowled over to his former corner and stood there, glaring at the production crew. They quickly found something to do and somewhere else to look.

Crossing his arms and returning to the piece of wall he'd been holding up, Zane didn't look at her, either, when he asked, "Want to talk about it?"

"Some days I want to kill him," she grumbled.

"I know."

"How do you stand him? How can you still be his friend after all these years?"

"Because he'd give me the shirt off his back if I needed it. Practically did. He's loyal to the people he cares about, Marcy. Trust me when I say you don't know the whole story."

She shot him a pointed look. "No one will tell me."

Zane raised his hands in an unarmed gesture. "Not my story to tell."

"He just…drives me insane. He knows how important this photo shoot is. And he knows what I went through to get this set up in time. If Colt and Lena were here, I might be tempted to wring their necks…."

"You know that's not true." Zane bumped her hip with his own, hoping to jar a smile from her. "You liked those two. And you could have refused to sell the photographs back to Colt. But you didn't. Admit it, you have a romantic soft spot beneath that drill-sergeant exterior."

The ghost of a smile played at the edges of her lips. "If you breathe a word of that to Simon, I'll kill you."

"I'm shaking in my shoes."

_1_

ZANE STARED OUT THE CLOSED window to the panoramic picture of tropical beauty and sighed. It was perfect and he was bored.

He shouldn't be. This laid-back, no pressure lifestyle was exactly what he'd signed up for—the complete opposite of the life he'd left behind.

For good reason.

He swiveled in his desk chair until his full attention returned to the bank of security screens that occupied the wall in front of him. He should probably run back the tapes to check those sixty seconds he'd been distracted. But he wouldn't. In the eighteen months he'd been on the island, not a single exciting thing had ever shown up on those screens.

And why would it? The resort—the only thing on Île du Coeur—might have plenty to take, but there was only one way off the island. The chances of a thief being caught before the ferry arrived were pretty damn good. Especially with him on the job. None of their guests had ever had so much as a candy wrapper taken. The worst thing he'd had to deal with since he'd set foot

on the island was a drunk who'd fallen through one of
the thatched huts along the beach.

The only thing hurt had been the hut.

Zane looked at the timer in the bottom right corner
of one of the screens and registered that Tom, his replacement, would be there in about twenty minutes. So
far the boy was working out, and Zane was happy he'd
hired him.

After Tom arrived, Zane planned on walking the
grounds, checking that no guests from the couples side
of the resort had left their cabana doors standing open
in their romance-fueled haze.

The resort specialized in adult vacations. Singles
came not only to relax but to also meet other successful singles. They tended to stay in the main building
of the resort. Couples came for the romantic, secluded
atmosphere Escape excelled at creating. And since they
usually wanted more privacy, they occupied the bungalows on the far side of the resort. In between were various buildings and shared amenities—a bar, five-star
restaurant, gym and spa, water sports equipment and
instructors, tennis courts, a large pool complex and,
of course, the beach and jungle. Somehow the entire
resort managed to maintain an untouched, romantic
feel, while still offering the latest in modern amenities.

Part of that could be attributed to the remnants of the
French plantation house, the face of the entire complex.
The house itself had been expanded and updated over
the years, but it still retained the air of gentility and
mystery. The public rooms were more than two hundred
years old, keeping their period pine floors and rich in-
teriors. The guest rooms had been added on to the back
of the existing house at least fifty years ago when it had
first been converted to a resort. Since then, the struc-

tures had been updated and modernized several times over, the latest when Simon purchased the place.

After Zane had verified that everything and everyone was locked up tight, he was going to head to his own quarters at the back of the resort to see if there was anything interesting on TV.

That was his plan.

Until sirens began blaring overhead. Zane jackknifed in his chair, his eyes immediately sharpening and scanning the bank of monitors before him.

The information screen blinked *fire zone six* just as the telephone at his elbow rang. He punched a command into the system, his screens filling with every camera they had in zone six. Nothing. No flames. No smoke. All he saw was panicked guests running around. He shook his head at the pandemonium. Picking up the ringing line, he spoke to the nice woman from the alarm company on the other end.

Insurance required they maintain the service, although he had no idea why. No one from St. Lucia could get here in time to be of any help. Even with boats, it would take the fire department forty minutes to reach the island.

However, they were prepared. Even now, the head of the grounds crew was mobilizing the pump truck that they painstakingly tested once every month.

Not that Zane thought they'd need it.

Dropping the phone into the cradle, he immediately snatched it back up.

"Marcy, I don't see an actual fire. Evacuate the guests just in case, but I'm thinking this was either a short in the system or a drunken guest playing a prank."

"Zane, you know better than that. Our guests don't get drunk…they get happy."

"Yeah, yeah, feed me the line tomorrow, when I'm not dealing with a crisis."

The grumble in his voice belied the rush of adrenaline flowing through his veins…the first zing of electricity he'd felt in months. He'd missed it, this flurry of activity that meant he had a purpose.

"The staff is already implementing fire procedures. I'll let you know when all guests are accounted for," Marcy said.

"Let me know if anyone finds sign of a fire while you're at it."

Marcy chuckled.

Slamming down the receiver, Zane began to furiously type in commands, systematically scanning each zone, starting with five and seven before backtracking to one.

He didn't get much further.

Halfway through scanning the fourth-floor hallway, he watched a woman disappear inside one of the guest rooms.

"Idiot," he muttered under his breath. She'd obviously heard the fire alarm. Hell, it was practically spiking into his brain and making his eyes throb. God only knew what she thought was more important than meeting a fiery death.

He was halfway out of his chair when she reappeared…and went to the door immediately to the right. Ten seconds flat and she was inside that room, too. Because the main guest rooms were housed in the old French plantation house, they didn't have modern keycard technology.

He'd argued with Simon about the need to upgrade to that sort of system but the other man had grumbled something about old-world charm and authenticity, tacking on a statement about cost and headaches. Zane had managed to talk Simon into adding security cards to the restricted areas and the executive suite on the top floor, but that was as far as he'd been able to push. He wondered if the man would listen to him now.

He watched the woman on his screen appear and disappear one more time. Alarm bells—the ones inside his head—started clanging. Something wasn't right.

Picking up the two-way radio beside him, he yelled into it for Tom. "Get your ass up to the Crow's Nest," he said, using their nickname for the security hub. "I've got a situation, but I want eyes up here in thirty seconds."

A crackle of static floated up from his hand as he raced into the stairwell. "But…"

"Now," he yelled again. Whatever the other man was doing could wait.

Zane's mind raced just as fast as his feet, putting the pieces together as he flew down the two flights of stairs.

The fire alarm had been a diversion.

He burst through the door just in time to see the red-haired woman slip into yet another room. He'd barely gotten three doors down when she reappeared.

"Hey! Stop! What are you doing?"

Zane reached automatically to his hip, searching for a piece of his past that was no longer there. He hadn't felt the need for a sidearm in almost two years.

His body tensed for the chase. He expected her to run—they always did. Instead, she stopped in her tracks and turned to face him.

"Thank God." He could see tears glistening in the corners of her eyes as she took a step toward him. Warily, he slowed.

"What are you doing?"

"I was looking for my room, but I couldn't find it and the alarm is making my head hurt and I started to panic and…"

Her rambling words trailed off as one of those tears slipped free and rolled down her cheek.

He might have bought it, if he hadn't seen her go in and out of several locked rooms with his own eyes. With a speed that would make his trainer at The Farm weep.

He went to step behind her and she spun, her eyes going wide and her mouth opening in a silent protest.

"Turn around."

"Wait. Why? What are you doing?"

He took out his badge—nothing like the one he used to carry, this one was white plastic with his picture and title as head of security for the resort in big, bold letters—and held it in her face so she could get a good look at it. "Turn around before I put your face in the wall."

Reluctantly, she took a half step sideways, presenting him with just enough of her arm to grasp and spin. Snatching the other one, he had her wrists locked into one hand and his other pressed between her shoulder blades, just enough to keep her uncomfortable and co-operative but not enough to damage.

"Now, we're going to take a little walk. And you're going to tell me exactly what you stole from those rooms—" he couldn't help himself, he really wanted to know her secret "—and how you got in and out so fast."

"I swear, I didn't steal anything."

"We'll see about that."

WELL, SHE OBVIOUSLY HADN'T gotten away clean. Giselle Monroe wanted desperately to rub the throbbing pain centered right between her eye sockets, but she couldn't. Her wrists were currently locked together behind her and tethered to a rickety chair. Her mind flashed back to the one other time she'd felt the cold steel of handcuffs against her skin. Not her finest hour.

She'd been sixteen, rebelling against her overprotective father and brothers—all three of whom were cops—and had been caught, breaking into the school gymnasium with her friends. They'd honestly been doing it for a lark, nothing else. The fact that the cop hadn't found any spray paint or drugs or anything else had gone a long way in getting them community service and two weeks suspension instead of a stiffer sentence from the courts and the school.

Well, that and the pull of her family's name.

For a teenager, community service had been bad enough. When her father had found out she was the one who'd picked the lock, he'd tacked on six months' house arrest. Sneaking in and out of the house had become a skill she learned for survival during those months.

Her father would be so proud to see how she'd put those old skills to new use. The sarcasm and cold metal cut into her skin, reminding her she was far away from home, with no father or brothers to save her this time. But she wasn't about to show the tight-jawed giant who'd unceremoniously dumped her here any weakness, especially the fear snaking through her belly.

Okay, so her assessment of him might be a bit unfair, considering the guy was just doing his job, but he'd locked her inside a closet-size room with stale air and the permeating smell of industrial-grade cleaners. And then left her here. Alone.

She had no doubt that she was being watched. She could practically feel his eyes on her. Waiting for her story to crumble.

The beauty was that it wouldn't.

By now, he'd probably questioned the guests of the rooms she'd been in and discovered that nothing had been taken…because she hadn't been lying. She hadn't broken into the rooms because she'd wanted to steal anything, and certainly not from the guests. Recover what was rightfully hers? Absolutely. Steal? She wasn't a criminal. There was a difference, not that the Wall of Silence was likely to understand that.

The door squeaked open.

Without turning around, she asked, "Are you going to let me out of here?"

"Probably not."

"Wha—" she squeaked, craning around in the chair as far as the handcuffs at her wrists would let her. "What do you mean 'probably not'? I didn't steal anything. You have no right to hold me!"

Elle rattled the metal rings against the wooden slats of the chair, using their noise to punctuate her protests. "The minute you let me out of here, I'm calling my lawyer. I'll own this place when I'm done."

Which would actually make her search measurably easier. For a brief moment, she indulged the vision of booting everyone off the island so that she could run from one room to the other until she found the painting of her grandmother that her sleazy ex-boyfriend had stolen from her four years ago.

The piece was far from priceless, at least in art circles. It had been semivaluable. The man who'd painted it, a lover from her grandmother's own misspent youth, had achieved a moderate amount of success after their

time together. The painting had gone up in value some-
what over the years, but the emotion behind it had
always meant more to Elle.

The colors were lush. Burgundy, gold, black, green.
Her grandmother, a young woman just beginning to
taste the world, was looking over her bare shoulder,
caught in the act of dropping her robe to the ground.
The mischief and passion in her bright gray eyes, so
familiar and yet so different, had always called to Elle.
Nana had never married the man. In fact, she'd gone on
to devote her life to someone else. Very happily, to hear
her tell it, although Elle had never met her grandfather.
But caught in that one moment of time, there was no
mistaking that the young woman her grandmother once
was desperately desired the man staring at her with a
brush in his hand.

The painting was the one and only possession of
her grandmother's that she'd had, but it was also so
much more. The skill of the painter was evident in
the layering of color, the shadow and light. The way
he'd captured the hint of daring in the sparkle of her
grandmother's eyes. That image had been evidence to
a struggling teenage girl that the world didn't revolve
solely around strict rules and unbreakable laws. It had
been proof that there was a world outside her father's
house, one she'd someday get to experience, just as her
grandmother had.

Nana had been the only female influence in Elle's
life after her mother had died when she was very young.
She'd also been the only one to understand Elle's reckless artistic bent and had encouraged her to explore her
talents. She wished Nana could see the success she'd
found in the past few years—the sale of her paintings
finally supporting her.

Nana had understood her. And for Elle, the painting represented that bond of understanding, as well.

She'd been heartbroken when, disgruntled over the fact that she'd kicked his sorry, mooching, jobless ass to the curb, Mac had ransacked her place, taking anything in her apartment worth more than a dime. Her computer, TV, DVD player...everything.

Although, all she'd cared about was the painting. It was the only thing that couldn't be replaced.

Mac had disappeared along with all of her stuff. She'd filed a police report, but she had enough cops in her family to realize her possessions had vanished right along with him. She'd wanted to protest as the officer who'd taken her statement had written down *miscellaneous wall art* when she'd listed her Nana's painting.

She'd cried herself to sleep that night, knowing it was gone forever.

But then eight weeks ago, she'd opened *Worldwide Travel* and seen the glossy picture of a resort and the painting of her seminude grandmother against the backdrop of lush green walls and sparkling ocean. She'd known she needed to get it back.

Her father and brothers had told her the foreign location of the resort made recovery next to impossible. The lawyer she'd consulted had said the same thing. Foreign courts were complicated enough, but she couldn't even prove the painting was hers. It had been gifted to her grandmother, who'd gifted it to her. There was no paper trail. She could prove that the painting was of her grandmother, but that didn't mean she'd ever owned it.

She'd thought to reason with the owner of the island. If he'd bothered to return any of her letters, emails or phone calls, she might not have had to resort to treachery in order to recover what was rightfully hers.

She had to assume that the owner knew the piece was stolen and had no intention of returning it to her.

That freed up her moral obligations to the commandment about stealing rather nicely. While Sister Mary Theresa wouldn't approve, Elle's conscience was clean.

A picture slammed onto the surface of the rickety table before her, pulling her from her self-righteous anger and making her jump. The handcuffs rattled again, only this time it wasn't for effect and the jarring sensation jolted up her arms and into her shoulders, making her want to double over—if she'd had the freedom of movement to do so.

It took her a moment to focus her attention on just what was sitting in front of her. Her eyes squinted at the grainy black-and-white image as a coil of unease began to tighten in her chest.

"I do have the right to hold you, considering this photo proves that you were the source of a false fire alarm. The same one you claimed made you disoriented and unable to find your own room."

Yeah. This was not good.

Elle fought the urge to open her mouth and let words start spilling out. She had no doubt the hard-ass who'd delighted in clamping her to this chair wouldn't understand why she was here or believe her without the proof her lawyer had pointed out she didn't have.

He rounded the table to stare across the scored and dirty surface and placed his palms flat onto the center, leaning forward into her space. Her only thought was *damn, the man is tall*. He was big, too, with broad shoulders and the kind of muscles that clothes couldn't disguise. Any other time, she'd have enjoyed staring at him.

At this precise moment, not so much.

"Feel free to call your lawyer. You won't get a damn thing."

His eyes bored into her and, for the first time since she'd come to the island, she began to squirm. They were a mix of green and gold and gray that shouldn't have been mesmerizing but somehow was. The expression in them was hard, disconnected almost. She'd seen that expression before, in her dad's eyes on the nights he'd come home late after working a particularly horrendous murder.

She licked her lips, fighting the urge to reach out to him in the same way she'd always tried to bring the light back into her dad's face. But this wasn't the time. And he wasn't her problem.

The silence stretched between them, broken only by the loud bang of the door as it slammed into the wall.

"Zane, what are you doing?"

His mouth pinched before his focus switched to the man who'd just entered.

"Questioning a thief."

"That's not what Marcy said. According to her, this woman didn't take a damn thing and we have no right to hold her."

"She pulled the fire alarm."

"I don't care if she put on a rabbit suit and paraded up and down the halls, pretending she was the Easter bunny. Let her go."

Elle craned her head around until she could see her would-be savior.

He wasn't what she'd expected. While the man's words had certainly been stern enough, his posture was anything but. He lounged against the open doorway, one hand lodged in a pocket at his hip and the other dangling loosely at his side. His shorts were slack around his hips. He had on a Hawaiian shirt, a dark cord of some kind wrapped around his tanned throat.

The man was the picture of laid-back island life. Elle thought it was a lie. A core of steel lurked somewhere deep inside. There was certainly no question he had some level of authority over Hard-Ass. She hoped he was about to use it to her advantage.

"Now, be a good boy and unlock those handcuffs before she calls her lawyer."

"She's already threatened to do that."

She watched as a grimace crossed his face. "I'm sure there's no reason for that. I apologize for Zane's behavior. He's ex-CIA."

He made the statement as if it explained absolutely everything there was to know about the other man. And dragging her gaze back over to him, she thought it just might.

Hard-Ass's…no, Zane's jaw tightened even more as he pulled a key from his pocket. His eyes stared down at it as if he wished for the ability to bend it and render it useless so he'd have a legitimate reason to keep her here against orders.

With heavy, reluctant steps, he walked behind her. Even though she couldn't see him, she knew that he towered above her. His long shadow dropped over the table, the curve of his head obscuring the single light from above.

His fingers wrapped around her elbow, smoothing down the inside curve of her arm until they slipped over the sensitive sweep of her wrist. A shiver of unwanted awareness spiked up her arm and into her body. She sucked in a breath at the unexpected reaction to the contact.

She was so unnerved that it took her several seconds

to register her freedom when the tension that had bound her wrists together finally disappeared. Elle shot from the chair, almost knocking over the table in her haste to get away from his intimidating presence behind her. She spun to face both of the men.

The contrast between them was astonishing. One had sun-kissed cheeks and a genuine smile, the other's face was tight with a frown of disapproval.

"There. That's better. Ms. Monroe, my manager has arranged for you to be upgraded to a suite. Your luggage will be moved shortly. If you need anything else during your stay, be sure to let Marcy know. Zane, behave."

Pushing up from his permanent perch at the door, the man offered his hand, which she reflexively took. He was gone before she realized she had no idea who he actually was.

Turning to the scowling man, she asked, "Who was that?"

"Your guardian angel apparently."

With the open door and the promise of no retribution for her stunt, Elle was feeling a bit cocky...cocky enough to do something she probably shouldn't have.

Turning her focus fully to the man left behind, she said, "My guess is he definitely has a higher security clearance than you."

Zane's jaw tightened and he took a menacing step toward her. Her bravado disappeared rather quickly when he entered her personal space. The cells in her body seemed to react, standing at attention simply because he was nearer to her. It was galling.

His huge hand wrapped around her arm once again, pulling her close enough to his body that she could feel the heat of him radiating into her own skin. His scent, dark, spicy and all male, filled her lungs despite the fact that she tried not to breathe.

"I am the highest security clearance in this place." His head dipped down toward hers and her lips parted automatically. His mouth brushed against the sensitive outer shell of her ear as he whispered, "And I'm going to be watching you. Wherever you go, whatever you do, I'm going to be watching."

A shiver of awareness, anger and anticipation racked her body even as she jerked her arm from his grasp. He easily let her go.

Elle schooled her features and looked up into his face. "Then it's going to be a boring week for you."

"For your sake, I hope so."

2

ZANE WATCHED AS THE WOMAN walked away. The taunting swing of her hips and the way she tossed her red hair behind her as she threw a knowing half smile over her shoulder made his fists clench.

He stomped down the hall after her. Not to bring her back, but to give Simon a piece of his mind. He was pissed, and someone was going to get the brunt of his anger.

His knock on the suite door was perfunctory to say the least. He didn't bother waiting for Simon to acknowledge him before he pushed into the other man's domain.

The living area before him was immaculate, not a single thing out of place. Of course, that had absolutely nothing to do with Simon and everything to do with his efficient director. He and Simon had shared an apartment during college, so he had firsthand knowledge of the man's messy gene. Not that he'd cared much back then. They'd both focused on women, partying and studying, in that order. There'd been little energy left over for domestic things such as scrubbing toilets or washing dishes.

Luckily Simon had an entire staff to do those things for him now.

Zane strode into the lion's den. That's what everyone liked to call it behind Simon's back.

Very few people ever saw the inside of his sanctuary. Simon liked his privacy, and Zane understood why. However, at the moment, the last thing Zane was worried about was protecting the sanctity of Simon's hidey-hole.

"Simon!" Zane bellowed walking into the center of the room.

"Took you longer to get here than I expected."

Simon's slow drawl came from behind. Zane spun in surprise and immediately felt his body falling into a fighting stance. He was going soft, if Simon could startle him.

"What the hell are you doing? She started a false fire alarm. She might not have stolen anything—yet—but she did break into several guest rooms. And you're rewarding her with an upgrade? I can't do my job if you countermand every decision I try to make."

Simon walked across the smooth wooden floor to a bar set into the far wall. Leaning over and reaching behind it, he pulled out two glasses and a bottle of brandy. "Want some?"

"No, I do not want a drink!"

He shook his head, frowning and said, "You really should relax more, Zane. You're going to have a heart attack before you're forty."

The dark amber liquid splashed into the bulb of the glass. "As we speak, her bags are being transferred to the Crow's Nest, where you can look through them before sending them to her new room. And I'm surprised you haven't realized that the room I upgraded her to happens to be located in a corner and covered by two more cameras than her previous location."

Simon looked up at him, narrowing his eyes over the edge of the glass as he took a sip. "*You're welcome.* Hey, look, I managed to play the good cop to your bad cop. Without any training, too."

Great. He'd gone from working for the CIA to playing cops and robbers with a man who had a Peter Pan complex. Never mind that Simon had made a smart move. One Zane should have thought of. He really was getting soft.

Simon clapped his hand on to Zane's shoulder. "Give it a rest, man. Didn't your mom ever tell you not to frown? Your face could stick that way."

"I'm not frowning."

"The hell you say. I've known you for how long?"

"Too long," Zane mumbled.

"Exactly. I can tell the minute you start castigating yourself. You get this really ugly furrow in the center of your forehead. Used to get the same thing when I went after some girl you liked at the bar."

Zane growled deep in the back of his throat. A warning they both knew Simon would ignore. Their relationship had always been complicated. They annoyed the hell out of each other, had always been competitors for everything and each would take a bullet for the other without a second thought. Neither of them had siblings, and Zane often thought they filled that role for each other.

Simon pulled no punches, and Zane trusted him to tell the truth…whether he wanted to hear it or not.

Zane turned to leave. He was halfway out before Simon's voice stopped him.

"Let me know if you find any red lace panties. I could use a little distraction right now. That woman is quite a firecracker, and I wouldn't mind getting a little singed."

Zane's hands wrapped into fists as he spun on his heel. Simon lounged against the bar, a taunting half smile and a twinkle in his eye. Zane relaxed his body again.

"Bastard."

The man had always known which buttons to push.

ELLE RUMMAGED FRANTICALLY through her luggage, looking for the picture she'd torn from the magazine. She'd been staring at it every night for the past two months and now that she couldn't find it, panic began to rise in her chest. She needed that picture. It held the only clues she had to finding her grandmother's painting.

She tore into her suitcase, flinging clothing every which way, hoping that she'd simply missed it the first time.

She never should have let them touch her things!

A warm wave of relief flooded through her. There, placed neatly at the very bottom of her suitcase sat what she was looking for. Picking it up, Elle ran the pad of her thumb across the glossy image. How had she missed it the first time?

The picture was fairly large, taking up most of the space on the page.

She had to admit, the ad had done its job. She'd wanted to come to Escape even before she'd noticed the painting hanging on the wall in the background.

The vista the camera lens let the audience into was

just as breathtaking as the lush tropical surroundings that stood outside the walls. The angle the photographer had chosen accentuated the perspective, elongating the lines of the comfortable living room, through what she assumed was a bedroom and out the floor-to-ceiling windows to the ocean beyond.

All of the furniture was heavy wood, looking as if the pieces had stood there through years of love and use. Tranquil blues and greens decorated the walls and dotted every surface. And in between two towering bookshelves hung the painting of her grandmother, somehow even more lavish surrounded by the tropical beauty outside.

The artist in Elle could appreciate the composition and structure of the photograph. The way the photographer had staged the shot to convey a feeling of lush peace and beauty. The little girl she'd never really got to be wanted the only memento of her grandmother back so desperately her lungs tightened with the need to run screaming through the place, ripping doors open until she found what she'd come for.

But that would just land her back inside the dank, cramped space with Officer Zane standing over her, asking questions she really didn't want to answer.

Instead, she concentrated on trying to find some clue within the picture. A clue she hadn't found the hundreds of times she'd stared at it before.

The entire resort had a sort of lived-in feel, as if you were vacationing with a long-lost aunt who just happened to be a billionaire. Each of the guest rooms that occupied the French plantation house was decorated differently…which should have made her search easier, but so far hadn't. Yes, she'd been able to glance into each of the rooms she'd seen and know whether or not it was *the one*. But there were so many of them and she had no way to narrow down her search. Not to mention that once she had searched the rooms inside, she had to cover all of the bungalows reserved exclusively for couples, the common areas and the restricted spaces.

She hadn't gotten into nearly enough rooms today. And to make matters worse, she had no doubt that Zane had been telling the truth and would be watching her every move now.

Elle sighed, mentally rearranging her schedule in her head. She had a couple of commissioned paintings she should be working on, but both clients could be put off for a little while. An Atlanta gallery had expressed interest in a showing. But that was months away. Really, there were worse places on the planet to be stuck than an exotic Caribbean island.

The place was stunning. And her upgraded room had a killer view.

Unfortunately, it didn't contain her grandmother's painting, either. That would have made her life too easy.

Flopping back onto the bed, she let her body sink into the luxurious comforter. She stared up at the beautiful crown molding that ringed the ceiling and, for the first time, admitted she hadn't exactly planned. She could hear her dad's voice in her head now. "You went off half-cocked again, didn't you, girl?" Even in her own brain, the stern voice couldn't disguise the indulgent humor beneath.

So, she was guilty of rushing into things, of responding passionately to a situation before she'd fully thought out the consequences. There were certainly worse ways to interact with the world. She could have a stick up her ass like Officer Zane. She'd bet he thought out every angle for absolutely every decision before he took a single step.

Mind-blowing.

A vision of him standing over her flitted through her mind. Unwanted warmth snaked through her body to pool between her thighs. So he was…ruggedly handsome. That didn't give him the right to push her around the way he had. Well, okay, maybe he did have the right, but she wasn't about to admit that out loud. She forced the image of his towering body and tight jaw out of her mind. She didn't have time to indulge in pointless yearnings.

What she needed was a plan.

And in the absence of one, a margarita. Or five. The answer would come to her. It always did.

"YOU SHOULD TAKE A break."

"No." Zane didn't even bother turning around to look at Marcy. His eyes were glued to the screen in front of him and the woman who currently filled it.

She'd been sitting at the bar for the past two hours. Alone. Sipping on several frothy drinks and ignoring the several men who had tried to pick her up.

"She isn't going anywhere, Zane. The last ferry has run for the day."

"I promised I'd be watching her and I intend to do just that."

"Who'd you promise? We both know Simon didn't ask you to do this. Leave the poor woman alone."

Poor woman, his left nut. The screen might have washed everything to varying shades of gray and white, but his mind remembered the vivid color of her hair and the unsettling combination of her gray eyes. They were so pale. So piercing. And they hid a secret he was determined to figure out.

"Don't make me put you on administrative leave for the next forty-eight hours."

His head whipped around to look at the compact fireball of a woman standing behind him. No doubt about it, Marcy was small but she packed a hell of a punch. And they both knew she didn't bluff worth a damn. If she said it, she meant it.

Zane thought about threatening her with Simon, but decided not to. Technically Simon might own the place, but everyone knew that Marcy ran it. He had no desire to get on her bad side by throwing his friendship with their boss in her face. Besides, he wasn't entirely certain that Simon would choose him over Marcy. After all, he could find another head of security tomorrow, but Marcy…she'd be damn hard to replace.

He was curious, though. "Why would you do that?"

"So that my week doesn't go to hell because you're bored and can't admit that you miss your old life."

"I do not miss my old life." Rather, there were things about his old life that he didn't miss, such as seeing murdered bodies or chasing terrorists and drug dealers and rapists. And knowing that for every bad guy they caught, another was ready to step up and take his place.

The guilt of knowing he'd failed Felicity, his fiancée, had been the last straw. Her death was entirely his fault and there was nothing he could do to change it.

"It does not escape my notice that you didn't protest being bored. I'm sending Tom in here in five minutes. If I don't see you walking through this doorway, heading to your own cottage five minutes after that, then consider yourself benched."

Zane fought the urge to grumble as Marcy disappeared and he waited for Tom to arrive. Now that he'd been booted, he could admit that his eyes were starting to sting from watching the grainy screen for hours.

He scanned all six of the monitors, taking in the normal vista of swaying palm trees, necking couples, and water lapping against sand. Until his gaze returned to the picture of Giselle Monroe. As he watched, yet another guy drunk with rum-soaked bravado sat on the bar stool beside her. Zane could see the man's mouth moving.

Giselle flicked her gaze to the guy for no more than half a breath before dismissing him again. She didn't even bother wasting words, simply shook her head in response to whatever the young buck had asked her.

Zane almost felt sorry for the guy as he stood from the bar and walked back to the cluster of his friends, to be razed for the rest of the night, Zane had no doubt.

She'd been doing that all evening. What kind of woman came to a singles resort specifically designed to facilitate vacation flings and then turned down every man who made a pass at her?

One who wasn't here for a hookup, obviously. So what was she here for? The question he desperately wanted an answer to burned inside his chest.

The lock clicked behind him, signaling that Tom had arrived to relieve him from the Nest.

Zane quickly made a decision. What could it hurt if he stopped at the bar himself just to check on things? After all, it was his job to make sure all ran smoothly.

DAMN, SHE WAS TIRED OF fending off drunk men. If one more guy came up to her with some lame pickup line and an offer to "fulfill all her fantasies" she was going to knock someone's block off.

All around her, desperate women in skintight cloth-ing, inch-thick makeup and sky-high heels giggled and hair tossed. Pathetic.

She could feel the presence of another male as he slid onto the empty stool beside her. It had been vacant most of the night. And that's how she preferred it.

Without turning around, she said, "Don't bother. I'm not interested. Try the blonde at the other end of the bar."

That one was definitely looking for a quick lay... probably with more than one man. Possibly at one time.

"Does that mean you won't accept my apology drink?"

Her head whipped around. The dark voice slipped down her spine as if he'd dropped an ice cube straight from the drink in front of him down her exposed nape.

He still had on the same clothes—dark black jeans and a tight black T-shirt—but somehow he looked more laid-back than he had before. Maybe it was just the change in scenery. Everything looked laid-back with a thatched roof over your head and a fruity drink in your hand. As opposed to adorned with handcuffs inside a utility closet.

"No, thank you."

Her voice was tighter than she'd meant it to be. He was making a peace offering, after all. But it was hard to take the gesture at face value. He was up to some-thing and she wouldn't put it past the hard-ass she'd met earlier today to slip something into her drink. Like truth serum.

Elle deliberately turned her head away, presenting him with her back, as she'd done with every other man who'd sat beside her tonight. Unlike the rest of them, Officer Zane settled into the chair anyway, throwing his arm over the rounded edge of the back and signaling to the bartender. Magically another of the frothy pink concoctions she'd been drinking all night appeared at her elbow.

She frowned, throwing a daggered look over her shoulder. "You don't take *no* very well, do you?"

"Not usually. And you don't mingle very well." He threw a hand out behind them, gesturing to the crowd of rowdy twenty- and thirtysomething singles laughing and having a good time.

"Maybe I just don't feel like chatting right now."

"What kind of woman comes to a resort that specializes in providing fertile hunting grounds for prowling singles, and doesn't bother to actually prowl?"

A flush of anger and embarrassment suffused her skin and, before she could stop herself, she swung around in her chair to fully face him.

"I don't know. The kind who had her hands unjustly handcuffed to a chair a few hours ago. Let's just say, I'm not exactly in a partying mood."

"Oh, we both know my actions were justified."

"So much for that apology."

He shrugged. "I tried."

"Let me guess, the mystery man made you do this. I bet it galls the hell out of you that he believes me."

Elle's gaze strayed to his lips as they twisted momentarily into a grimace. There was something enticing about the expression, about the way his upper lip was slightly larger than the bottom and the corners pulled down even when he wasn't frowning. Which, from what she'd seen, wasn't very often.

"Jeez, you guys are all the same."

"And what's that supposed to mean?"

"The minute they tell you they don't need you on

the force anymore—you're too old, you're injured, you made some bonehead mistake—you all turn mean and nasty. Can't stand to sit with your hands under your ass, useless and restless."

He raised a single eyebrow, but didn't say anything.

"So, what was it? My guess is you got shot, because you're way too young to be benched at a desk, and despite the fact that you're acting outside of orders at the moment, you're too by the book for a bonehead mistake."

She regretted the words almost the minute they left her mouth. She looked into his eyes and saw the pain lurking there, deep in the back. She'd hit her mark, all right and injured an already wounded man.

She didn't want to feel guilty, not about hurting the good officer. But she couldn't help it. She'd grown up around guys exactly like him. They were all tough as nails. Until they weren't.

"I'm sorry." The words were low as they left her lips. Part of her hoped the loud music and laughing crowd would drown them out. The other part knew she wouldn't sleep tonight because of the guilt if he didn't hear them.

"I'm sorry," she said louder.

His eyes cut across at her from beneath smoky lashes. "I heard you the first time."

Elle sighed. "Yeah, well, I wasn't sure."

"Not your fault."

"Maybe." Picking up the glass in front of her, she threw it back and let the semimelted rum-soaked ice fill her mouth.

"You wanna make it up to me? Tell me what you were really doing this afternoon."

She wasn't feeling that guilty.

"I already told you."

"And we both know that was a lie."

This time, it was her turn to shrug.

"Then I guess you're just going to have to add this to your long list of disappointments."

Elle pushed up from the bar, ignoring the way it spun lazily around her. She wobbled on her low-slung heels for a moment before the world finally righted itself.

"Are you okay?"

Before she could blink, Zane was standing beside her, his hand wrapped around her elbow again. The moment felt like déjà vu in a not very pleasant way.

Jerking her arm out of his grasp, she said, "I'm fine."

So the—one, two, four, five? Dang, she'd had more than she'd realized—fluffy drinks that had seemed rather harmless while sitting down had gone to her head. She had only a short walk to the main building and a ride in the elevator before she could crash in her own room and sleep off the alcohol haze. Maybe when she woke up, she'd have a brilliant solution to her problem.

"At least let me walk you to your room."

"I don't think so." Giving him her back, she strode away.

Outside the bar, the salt-tinged air began to clear her head. It was a beautiful night, the slivered moon just barely gilding the silky sand and the crystal-clear water.

What she wouldn't give to have a paintbrush in her hand right now. To capture the beauty of this place forever.

The loud music and bright lights of the bar faded, leaving her feeling alone in the tropical paradise. If she'd been here for any other reason, she might have enjoyed the sense of peace that stole over her. It was an unexpected gift at the end of a rather trying day.

Stopping in the middle of the deserted path, she closed her eyes and breathed in the perfectly warm air.

A burst of laughter from behind galvanized her into motion again.

The sandals she'd thrown on only because they matched her sundress clicked loudly against the concrete path. So loudly that it took her a minute to pick up the sound of the second pair of footsteps following behind her. They were quiet and, if her own overprotective father hadn't trained her, she probably never would have picked up on them. But, living in Atlanta, her daddy had made sure she was always aware of her surroundings and could defend herself.

Her sluggish brain reacted a little slower than she would have liked, but it took her only a few moments to assess the situation. She was alone on a dark path, surrounded by thick landscaping and plenty of nooks and crannies that could be used to pull her into the shadows.

The parade of men she'd grown increasingly harsher with as the night had gone on marched through her brain. Crap, she should have been nicer.

3

ZANE TAILED ELLE. FOLLOWING her had nothing to do with suspicions and everything to do with the fact that she'd looked less than steady on her feet back at the bar. She might have regained her balance fairly quickly, but he wasn't in the habit of letting drunk women walk home alone.

That was just asking for trouble. He'd worked enough cases with female victims who had been in the wrong place at the right time and ended up dead. And while the likelihood of that happening in this tropical paradise was fairly low—thanks to the security measures he'd implemented—he still wouldn't be able to sleep tonight if he'd let her walk out of that bar on her own.

The path back to the main building was long, and he suddenly felt responsible for Elle. God only knew why.

He rounded a corner on the path, realizing too late that the click of her footsteps ahead of him had gone silent.

The attack came out of nowhere. If he hadn't been preoccupied with worrying about Elle, it never would have happened. Two years ago, his brain would have noticed the lack of sound, calculated the most-likely position where she'd gone off the path and prepared for any number of things—including the possibility that she might attack him.

Tonight, he was caught off guard as she came hurdling toward him out of the bushes. Her lithe body became a projectile headed straight for his chest. He had no desire to fall over backward from the force of her attack.

Defensive moves that had long ago become instinctive kicked in. He sidestepped the motion of her body, reaching out to try to stop her forward momentum. He might have no desire to hit concrete, but then he really didn't want her to, either. Too much paperwork involved.

His fingers slid across her dress, fighting for purchase. He could feel the angle of her body shift beneath the slippery fabric as she countered his attempt to save her. The sound of cotton rending ripped through the air, mixing with the loud expulsion of her breath close to his ear. Her shoulder glanced off of his arm, the strength of her tiny body surprising him.

Elle went off balance. He knew the second that her center of gravity overcorrected itself and couldn't recover. He knew because he watched as her eyes, more cognizant than he'd expected, widened in panic.

He lunged for her, but it was too late. If she'd still been standing on the path, he might have been able to grasp her and roll them both so she landed on top of him, shielding her from most of the impact. But the little minx had laid her trap right next to the pool.

"Elle!" He cried out a warning she obviously didn't need.

He probably could have saved himself the dunking if he'd pushed against her momentum, but he didn't. Instead, he tried to pull her in close to his body so that he could find her once they disappeared beneath the surface.

Neither of them was in danger of drowning. They might have landed in the deep end of the pool, but it was only six feet. Elle was tiny, but surely she could find her way to the surface with little effort, even if she had been drunk and disoriented. And considering the dexterity she'd needed for her botched attack, he was seriously reconsidering his assessment of her ability to hold liquor.

Warm water closed over his head. Chlorine stung his eyes as he kept them open, not willing to take his gaze off of Elle until he knew she was okay.

Her feet touched down against the tiled bottom of the pool, pushing off in a way that had her dress floating precariously high up the smooth expanse of her thighs. Another reason to keep his eyes open. She shot past him like a seal.

He broke the surface in time to hear the gasp of her breath as her head cleared the waterline. She sputtered, her arms churning to keep from sinking again.

"What the hell!"

"I could ask you the same thing."

Elle spun around in the water to face him, the yellow material of her dress pooling around her body like a puddle of sunshine. Zane fought the urge to dunk his head back under.

"What did you think you were doing?" Zane demanded.

Anger began to mingle with the adrenaline in his blood. What had she been thinking? Had she known it was him on the path and intended to make him pay for locking her up earlier today? Or had she thought he was someone else, some other guy who was following her back to her room?

Either way, he was going to shake some sense into her.

"Defending myself," Elle said.

Zane reached for her, but before he could touch her, she kicked out with her legs and swam away.

She might be fast, but he was faster. Halfway across the pool, he caught her. Wrapping his arm around her waist, he yanked her to a halt. His feet found the bottom, standing them both up in waist-high water, although he didn't let her go.

"Defending yourself? Are you insane? You're, what, a hundred pounds soaking wet? You couldn't defend yourself against a fly, let alone a man who's probably close to double your weight."

Her eyes narrowed. The gray irises glittered in the darkness. They reminded him of the moon above their head, not as it was now, a sliver, but when it was full and bright.

"Hasn't anyone ever told you size doesn't matter?"

She wanted to squirm in his grasp. He could see the desire to fight for freedom lurking in her eyes. The fact that she fought against it, knowing it wouldn't do her any good, impressed him. Most people would have let instinct overrule intelligence and struggle anyway.

He pulled her closer, both because the need to feel her body against his was overwhelming and because he wanted to see her reaction.

"Honey, size always matters. We both know I could hold you under this water, drown you, with little effort."

He let his words sink in. Hoped they would sink in, before adding, "If I wanted to."

The smirk that touched her lips for a brief second told him his threat hadn't done a damn bit of good. Not only was she a firecracker, she was hardheaded, as well. He was about to give her a physical demonstration— nothing dangerous, just a quick dunking to prove he was right, but something else happened instead. She wasn't the one with her head dipping beneath the water.

In one quick burst of movement, she had his feet knocked out from under him and her hands covering the crown of his skull under the surface.

He didn't stay down long. She might have surprised him, but she couldn't keep him there—not that she'd tried. Instead, she stood her ground, her face bland and expectant as he bobbed back up.

"You were saying."

Okay, so maybe he'd underestimated her. The breaking and entering should have been his first clue, but skill with a lock didn't necessarily parlay into the ability to defend herself.

"Where'd you learn that?"

"I grew up the only female in a household of three cops—two brothers and a father. Would you let your little girl out in Atlanta without some basic training?"

A shiver raced down Zane's spine. He wasn't sure if it was the thought of her alone on the streets of Atlanta late at night, or in secret solidarity with anyone who'd risk threatening this little ball of energy under the misguided notion that she'd be an easy target.

"Point taken."

She smiled. This time, it wasn't a taunting gesture but one of understanding. Without another word, she turned and crossed the rest of the pool. Climbing up the tiled steps at the shallow end, she stood at the edge.

For the first time since she'd left the bar, he really looked at her. She was beautiful. And bedraggled. Her hair, normally bright was now dark with water. It dripped from the ends, making a gentle plopping sound as each drop hit the concrete deck.

Turning to face him, she tipped her head sideways and began to wring water from her hair. A puddle spread at her feet, turning the sun-baked concrete dark.

He'd half expected her to have mascara and other makeup streaking her face, but she didn't. Her dark lashes were absolutely natural.

Straightening up, she looked down at herself, lifting her hands and shaking them. A spray of water followed the gesture.

"I hope you're happy. I liked this dress. And these shoes will never be the same."

She looked back down at him as he stood mute in the center of the pool. His brain and his gaze were lost somewhere between the wet material that clung to her breasts and the shadowy triangle at the juncture of her thighs made by the skin-hugging fabric.

Her nipples puckered in the cool night air. He could see the way they peaked against the wet fabric. His mouth went bone-dry and his cock hardened to half attention. Shaking his head, he tried to ignore the normal physical response—hers and his. It didn't matter that his brain told his anatomy she was responding to the temperature, not him. He hadn't taken a lover in almost two years…since Felicity died.

Until tonight, he hadn't realized it had been that long. He definitely needed to get laid.

"Why were you following me?"

"I told you I'd be watching."

"Yes, but I thought you meant with those high-tech cameras mounted all over this place. I didn't think you were actually going to stalk me."

"Not stalk, follow. There's a difference."

"Tell that to my shoes."

Turning on her heel, Elle let out a resigned sigh. A shower of droplets arched behind her. Zane figured she'd probably have appreciated the effect if she could have seen it.

Her feet squelched in her shoes. The sound and the sight of her made his lips twitch against the urge to bust out laughing. Something told him she wouldn't appreciate that right now.

A trail of water was left in her wake, like the line a snail left behind when it moved. Trudging his way across the pool, he followed her, happy that the almost laughter seemed to have relieved the pressure of an erection he had no desire she become aware of.

"At least your shoes are open toed. I have on socks. Do you know how uncomfortable they are once they've soaked up half the pool?" he called out to her.

She threw a glare over her shoulder. "Nope, and I really don't care."

His lips twitched again.

She was five feet away from the path that lead toward the plantation house when she stopped suddenly in her tracks. Without turning around, she asked, "Well, are you coming? If you're going to follow me, I'd rather you do it in the open so I can avoid another unexpected swim."

She waited patiently for him to join her. As he walked up beside her, he couldn't help but notice the way her back straightened. Or the soggy dress as it clung to the curves of her ass.

A maze of unexpected reactions and contradictions burst through his body. He was attracted to her. Considering he hadn't found anyone attractive—including the half-naked women who paraded around this place all the time—since Felicity, he wasn't sure what to do with that knowledge.

No, he did. Nothing. It was chemical. Or biological. Or some other-ical that he'd never understood in college.

He found himself unnervingly intrigued by Elle Monroe. And considering he knew she was up to no good, that probably wasn't an intelligent reaction.

ELLE HATED THAT SHE WAS dripping all over the lobby floor. While the place was clearly a hotel, it also retained the air of someone's home, which came from its previous life as a working cocoa plantation.

It just went against the manners Nana had drilled into her brain. But the woman behind the desk smiled as she walked past, not even flinching at her bedraggled state. She supposed the front-desk clerk had seen plenty of shocking things at Escape…especially if she usually worked the night shift.

Elle watched as the woman's expression changed the minute Zane walked in behind her. Purely from objective observation, Elle recognized the feminine interest in the woman's eyes. How her dark brown irises sharpened.

"Zane. You're out and about late tonight." His shoes squeaked loudly against the highly polished wood floor. "Wet."

Elle heard the barely suppressed giggle in the woman's voice and fought the urge to snarl.

"We had a small mishap at the pool."

"Should I call Marcy?"

"No!" The word burst from both of them at the exact same time. The last thing she wanted was to have to explain how both she and the head of security had ended up wet. Together.

Without another word, they continued past the reception desk and into the hallway. Elle reached for the up button by the single elevator, but before she could punch it, Zane's hand was wrapped around her elbow again.

It was a nasty habit she was definitely going to have to break him of.

Zane steered her down the quiet hallway, toward a door marked Staff Only. Pulling a key card from his pocket, he unlocked the door, saying, "Faster."

The elevator he unceremoniously pushed her into spit them both out directly across from the door to her room. She'd looked at the door they walked out of several times and could have sworn it housed another suite...definitely not a freight elevator.

The building did have a few mysteries.

This time, it was her turn to yank out her key. Once the lock disengaged, Elle maneuvered herself so that her body stood between Zane and her open doorway.

That didn't stop him from peering in. And then pushing inside. "Jesus. Someone's ransacked your room. What did they take?"

Zane shoved her behind the towering wall of his body. His palm stayed wrapped around the jutting bone of her hip. The heat of his hand soaked through the suddenly cold material suctioned to her skin. A wave of awareness rolled through her.

It took her several seconds to register his words and see the room through his eyes.

"Nothing." Elle batted his hand away, both for the liberation and as a reminder that she really didn't want his hands on her. She didn't.

"I was…looking for something before I went down to the bar."

Zane turned to stare at her, genuine bafflement written all over his face. "What? The Hope Diamond? This place is a mess."

Elle spun around slowly, taking in her toiletries spread out across the top of the antique dresser. The way her jewelry spilled out of the little pouch she kept it in, one of her favorite necklaces hanging half in and half out. Reaching over, she pushed it back inside. One of her shirts hung over the arm of a chair. Another rested in a heap on the floor beside it. Her silky half-length robe fluttered against the porcelain washbasin that stood in the corner.

She shrugged. She was used to living inside chaos. It came with the territory. When inspiration struck, she dropped everything to paint or sculpt or draw or whatever.

She had to admit that the room looked a little worse than normal, thanks to her earlier scavenger hunt. But she was always one to acknowledge her faults and being scattered was definitely among them.

"Let me guess, your room is spotless. I bet there isn't even a speck of lint on the floor." *Regimented.* That was definitely a word she'd use to describe Agent Zane whatever. She had no idea what he'd done with the CIA, but all law-enforcement officers were pretty much the same.

And she admitted that part of her refusal to make the bed every morning stemmed from being forced to do it every day of her childhood. Rebelling was healthy... sometimes.

"Maybe."

However, in the face of his scrutiny, Elle found herself walking through the room, gathering her things so that she could dump them into the waiting suitcase. She did the same thing before her father visited. They now had an agreement. He called at least thirty minutes before he showed up at her door, and they both lived happily inside the illusion.

Besides, it wasn't as if she'd *expected* anyone to see her room this way. If she'd known a man was coming up... Oh, who was she kidding?

Zane stood in the center of the room and watched, his damp feet leaving a spot on the floor. Her hand touched the thin shell of her robe, reminding her that she was still wet and cold.

Spinning on her heel, she headed to the en suite, but realized that between the heavy antique furniture, her strewn luggage and the man standing in the center of her suite, she didn't have space to pass. Not without touching him.

Her nipples hardened at the thought, tingling as they'd done after she'd gotten out of the pool. The memory of his arm wrapped around her waist eased into her mind, like an old friend or the buzz from a perfect glass of wine.

Her breath hitched as her feet stopped just short of where he stood. Her clothes were extremely constricting. Zane stood before her, the flecks in his multicolored eyes glowing with the same awareness she was trying to deny.

Her tongue licked across her lips. She hadn't meant to do it, but they were suddenly so dry. His gaze snared on the motion. He didn't reach for her. He didn't have to. His tempting stare beckoned her to come just a little closer.

And she did, closing the space between them.

Their bodies didn't touch, and yet she could feel the heat of him. A shiver snaked down her spine, his warmth reminding her yet again that she was wet.

Her fingers suddenly itched to hold a charcoal pencil between them, to capture the expression of lust and awareness and male power that stretched his skin across the bones of his face. He was so beautiful in an unconventional way. And she had no doubt he'd protest at that word being used to describe him. He'd prefer rugged, hard, masculine, determined. And he really was all of those things. He held power, and the straight line of his shoulders said he knew it, and relished it. But the combination of sharp lines and arching curves, the perfect proportions pulled those rough edges together and softened them somehow into something very appealing.

And she noticed these things strictly from an artistic point of view of course.

Her eyes toured the length of his body. In for a penny, in for a pound. She appreciated that the strength of him carried all the way down. He was lean and powerful in a way that made her insides turn to mush. Normally, she would have said he wasn't her type. She tended toward guys with wiry frames and an artistic bent. It made things so much easier if she was with a man who understood her disposition. She'd learned over the years that it saved her heartache and headaches.

Zane reminded her of her father and brothers more than she wanted to admit. They were the same body type. The same personality. The kind of guy she steered clear of because she'd lived with him all her life and it hadn't gone well for anyone involved.

And yet, her blood chugged faster beneath her skin, picking up speed and heat and carrying oxygen laden with the smell of him to every cell in her body. Every inch of her would remember this moment long after it ended.

Her body moved of its own volition, yearning closer, wanting more of him. But she didn't close the gap.

Her lips parted. His warm breath brushed across her cheek, fluttering the tendrils of hair at her temple. They tickled her skin, but she wasn't laughing. His eyes held her in place, and she was unable to slip away or move closer.

They darkened with an awareness that echoed through her entire body. Her breath came increasingly faster, as if her lungs couldn't expand far enough to give her what she wanted.

And what she wanted was for him to kiss her. As much as she shouldn't. As much as that would complicate things beyond belief. Elle wasn't thinking about those things now.

A growl sounded low in his throat and a twist of desire arrowed to the center of her sex. She could feel the increasing ache, the wet slick that just anticipating his touch could produce.

But instead of finishing it, instead of grabbing her body and claiming her lips, Zane spun away and walked straight out her door without a backward glance.

She should be grateful that he'd had the brainpower

to realize giving in to the passion pulsing between them would be a stupid idea.

Instead, she was disappointed. And aroused. And pissed.

She wasn't used to men walking away. And she realized she didn't like it one little bit.

4

ELLE PUSHED HER TOES FARTHER into the cool sand. The beach was deserted. Most of the people on the island had no good reason to be up before sunrise. They'd come to relax and indulge, not rise with the chickens. She…she couldn't relax.

Erotic dreams, followed by tossing and turning and the lack of a solution for how she was going to find the painting had prevented her from getting more than a couple hours of sleep. She had no doubt there were bags under her eyes.

Not that there was anyone to notice.

If she had to be awake, though, she was going to take advantage of the moment. The quiet silence surrounded her. It was so different from home, where even in the early-morning hours there was activity on the street. Cars whizzing by, late-night revelers.

Atlanta might not be New York, but it was still a big city with constant motion. Normally, she liked that. She lived for it. For the excitement and the options and the possibilities. At home, she rarely sat still. There was just too much to do.

Which was why she was surprised to find herself enjoying simply resting on the sand. She pulled the sweater she'd thrown on over her shorts and tank top tighter around her body to ward off the early-morning chill. Closing her eyes, she tipped her face up as the first rays of sun touched her skin. A shiver ran through her, the sudden warmth startling.

The jungle that occupied the uninhabited side of the island started stirring with life. Behind her, birds began to sing. Insects buzzed. The island woke up. She'd come to this secluded stretch of the beach, as far away from the resort as she could get, on purpose.

Elle reached for the sketch pad and pieces of charcoal she'd placed beside her in the sand. She'd left home in such a hurry that she hadn't thought to bring her painting supplies. She'd been more concerned with recovering Nana's portrait than creating new ones.

She wondered languidly if the famed Marcy could get her some paint and brushes. The dawn light was perfect, but somehow sketching the wild surroundings just didn't do them justice. She needed a full palette to capture the richness of the colors around her.

She'd never be able to recreate them at home from her faulty memory.

When she'd come, she hadn't exactly expected to make this a working vacation. She'd hoped for a quick in and out.

A frown creased her forehead. Zane had pretty much made that impossible.

These moments right now were probably the only ones she'd get all day without his ever-watchful eyes on her.

Elle shook her head and concentrated on the sketch coming to life on the pad in front of her. The shading of the lush trees and sand in the rising sun. She smudged the line she'd drawn with the side of her hand, smearing the pencil to get the effect that she wanted. A trick she'd learned during her days at Savannah College of Art and Design. Her hand raced, quick and sure across the woven surface of the paper.

A bird, big with plumes of red and blue and green landed on a branch in the tree she'd been drawing. She quickly added it to the scene. Capturing the way it tilted its head, as if studying the creature invading its space.

As always, the entire world faded as Elle worked. She was absorbed in the moment and the race to capture the scene perfectly before the light changed.

The first clue that she wasn't alone was the rhythmic squelching of sand beneath pounding feet. She barely had time to jerk her head up before the spray of sand shot across the surface of her paper. Her eyes narrowed at the disturbance, she brushed the particles from her sketch and looked up at her intruder.

The sun was at his back, casting him in shadow and ringing him in a light that blinded her for a moment. But she didn't need to see his features to know who had disturbed her peace.

"Good morning, Officer Zane. You're out early."

"Special agent."

Elle frowned, not following him. "Huh?"

"I was a special agent, not an officer."

"What difference does it make?"

He chuckled. "A lot." When he dropped into a crouch beside her, Elle realized for the first time that he was almost naked, except for the navy blue nylon shorts and the expensive runners on his feet.

Despite the early-morning chill that still clung to the

air, his chest was wet with the evidence of his exertion. He was tanned and broad, the heavy muscles of his legs flexed against the strain of keeping himself balanced in a crouch. Although, that was the only evidence of any discomfort—the rest of him looked perfectly relaxed. Heaven only knew how long he'd been running on the sand to work up enough sweat to cover his body.

Probably a while.

A thrill raced down her spine and heat pooled in the center of her body. She could imagine working up a sweat with this man in another, better way. She wrinkled her nose at the inopportune thought.

"What have you got?" He reached for her sketch pad. With a squeal of protest, Elle scrambled to pull it out of his reach, but his reflexes were too fast. He had it in his lap, studying the picture—the unfinished picture—before she could stop him.

"This is really good."

"Don't sound so surprised," she grumbled. After a childhood of hearing that her art was just a hobby, useless and unproductive, she'd become overly protective of her work. She had a hard-and-fast rule that no one—not even Nana, when she was alive—saw her work in progress. It was private until she knew it was perfect and could share it with the world.

"You know, that was really rude. Most artists don't like to share their work until it's finished."

She watched, an unwanted knot lodged halfway between her stomach and her throat, as Zane cocked his head and studied her work in silence.

Finally, he looked up, a semismile curling the edges of his lips as he asked, "This isn't finished? It looks perfect to me. Amazing. How long did it take you to do this?"

A sort of euphoria bubbled up inside her. She tried hard not to smile back at him, to reward his rude behavior and "I own the world" attitude. But she couldn't help it.

"Um, about thirty minutes, I guess. I don't know. I left my watch back at the room."

"My God, that's amazing."

She shrugged, feeling her skin heat under the force of a blush. She never blushed.

Damn, this man was bad for her. He made her feel awkward and powerful and childish and hot all over. It had been a very long time since anything had made her feel awkward. She didn't like it. She'd learned early in life to fight for herself, against two older and stronger brothers, against a father who didn't understand her, against a world that thought becoming an artist wasn't a very smart choice.

She'd developed a thick skin. She'd had to in order to succeed and prove everyone wrong.

But apparently Officer Zane knew exactly how to get under that skin.

Handing the book back to her, he rose, his flexing thigh muscles impossible to ignore. She told herself she wouldn't have noticed if they hadn't been practically in her face.

"See you later."

The rising sun at his back blocked out the expression on his face, but she had no doubt that if she'd been able to see it she wouldn't have appreciated it. His tone of voice was rather smug.

"I'm sure you will."

He turned quickly, spraying sand in his wake. At least he waited until he was farther down the beach before he picked up the rhythm of his run.

Elle watched the wide V of his shoulders as they tapered down into the curve of his waist, the tight line of his butt and the give and take of his leg muscles as he headed back toward the resort.

And in that moment, the vision of that half smile curving his lips flashed across her mind. Without thought, she flipped to a clean page in her book and began drawing. She rarely sketched from memory, preferring to capture moments as they happened so she wouldn't forget anything.

The way he'd looked as he'd crouched beside her, the warmth that had suffused her body, that was something she wasn't likely to ever forget.

ZANE SHOOK THE WATER FROM his hair, swiping a towel over his damp body as he walked through his small bungalow. It wasn't much, a large open space that contained a bed, a couch and a TV. A stove he hardly ever used had been installed in the far corner, along with a few feet of cabinet space. There was no fresh market on the island, but there was a five-star restaurant right down the path, so cooking rarely seemed the best choice.

In the opposite corner, two beige walls boxed off the bathroom. At least his predecessor had thought to request a large tiled shower, complete with a glass-fronted view into the wild jungle that skirted the property. Simon sure as hell hadn't thought of that creature comfort on his own.

His place was set back from everything, giving him the illusion that he was on the island alone whenever he needed it. Simon lived in the middle of everything, not because he wanted to, but because he had to. Zane, on the other hand, preferred some space for when the memories and guilt got to be too much.

Today, the solitude might be what did him in. He'd caught himself staring out into the lush foliage...and remembering Elle sitting on the sand, her toes dug deep and her eyebrows beetled in concentration. He'd watched her for several minutes, unobserved, as she'd worked frantically to capture the unruly beauty of the jungle.

She'd done a damn good job of it, too.

It was unexpected. Not her drive...or her talent, if he'd thought about it. Elle struck him as the kind of person who would excel at whatever she put her mind to. She was feisty and determined. He'd seen enough to know she wouldn't accept anything less than perfection from herself. As much as it meant she would be a bigger pain in his ass, he admired her for that.

He hadn't figured her for the artistic type, though. A cat burglar? Sure. Not someone who captured the perfection of a moment the way she had this morning.

Now that he'd discovered that little tidbit of information, the question was, did it change anything? He didn't think so.

Elle Monroe was up to something. And he had every intention of finding out what. Back home, he'd have tapped her phones, set up surveillance, run background checks, gathered every speck of data he could find. He would have found her weakness and ruthlessly exploited it until he'd gotten the information he wanted.

The problem was that, here, he had no access to classified databases, no backup, no electronics. He was basically blind. Although, what he did have were some friends in the States. Friends who owed him. Friends he hadn't spoken to in eighteen months.

But he supposed they'd understand. They'd been there when Felicity died. Worked her crime scene. Told him she'd been pushed to her death by someone he knew…someone he'd tried to put away.

The guilt overwhelmed him. Eighteen months ago, that well of emotion would have had him reaching for a glass and a bottle. And slamming the phone back into the cradle because he couldn't face the pity that would be in the voice on the other end.

Today, he dialed.

"Mick, it's Zane."

Pressing the cordless phone to his ear, Zane walked lazily across the small expanse of his bungalow. He and the agent on the other end exchanged pleasantries. Mick tap-danced around asking the real question everyone wanted to know—how was he, and was he ever coming back?

Zane found himself staring through the bathroom, out the window and into the dank tangle of jungle beyond.

"Look, I need a favor. I need you to run a background check on Giselle Monroe. She lives in Atlanta. I think her father and brothers are all on the force there."

Zane listened for a moment, insulated from that jungle and the world in the silence he'd created.

He should have felt alone. He had every single day that he'd been here. Felicity gone, his life changed forever. No agents, no cases, no friends except for Simon. Nothing but the mundane ease of watching guests party and laugh and lie in the sun.

Today, he wasn't alone.

Today, he had the puzzle of Giselle Monroe. And he had every intention of having her…*solving* her. That's what he'd meant.

INSPIRATION HAD STRUCK AS Elle walked back through the hotel earlier that morning. She'd stopped in one of the small sitting areas off of the main salon. The clear light of an early-morning sun had been streaming in the windows that lined the space. The bright patches of yellow had illuminated several pieces of art lined up along the far wall.

They were brilliant pieces. None of them priceless masterpieces, but several by lesser-known painters from the twentieth and twenty-first centuries. Technique was difficult to miss, especially when she'd had it pounded into her head by brilliant teachers whom she'd wanted to kill at the time but now appreciated.

It had gotten her thinking. Whoever had decorated the place definitely had an appreciation for art. They knew the hidden gems. The brilliant pieces that didn't have a high level name and a higher-level price tag attached.

Surely this room couldn't be the only one to house a few paintings. Well, she knew it wasn't, because somewhere in the maze of rooms, buildings and bungalows another painting sat on another wall.

Could the solution to her problem be as simple as asking to see all of the art?

Once she figured out where the painting was, she could decide what to do next.

Stopping off at the front desk, Elle had asked to speak to Marcy. Considering it had barely been six-thirty, she'd expected to leave a message and receive a call from the woman later. To Elle's surprise, Marcy had materialized from a doorway behind the desk.

"What can I do for you, Ms. Monroe?"

It took Elle a few moments to order the thoughts in

her brain, to figure out the best way to ask her question without sounding too desperate, or tipping her hand.

"I was wondering if you could get something for me. From St. Lucia."

"I can certainly try. They don't have everything, but most things I can find. What do you need?"

"Painting supplies. A palette with pigments, a few brushes, an easel, a couple of canvases."

Marcy's eyebrows went up in surprise. Elle supposed her requests weren't the norm. Maybe vibrators and personal lubricants were what the front desk usually received requests for. Although, she'd bet the ever-efficient Marcy had those boxed and stacked in perfect order, just waiting to be wanted.

"Well...I have to admit, I'm not sure whether I can get those things, but I'll be happy to call over to our supplier and see what I can do. I'm sure you realize that they might be more expensive than you're used to paying at home."

Elle shrugged. She had struggled for years, but over the past couple of years had begun to do well. She had some mad money to play with. Besides, it was an investment. If she was lucky, she could not only find her grandmother's painting but also manage to produce a few of her own.

"I didn't realize the island would give me so much inspiration. I expected to find myself lying on the sand, a drink in my hand and fuzzy thoughts running through my brain."

Marcy smiled. "You strike me as the kind of woman who finds sitting on her rear dull...and impossible."

An answering smile touched Elle's own lips. "You know, I think you and I could be real good friends. If I wasn't going to be leaving soon."

"Something tells me you're right. I'll see what I can do."

"Thanks." She turned to leave, waiting until she was three steps away before turning back. "Oh, I noticed the artwork in several of the common rooms. I was wondering if maybe you had a tour of them. For guests?"

Marcy straightened her spine and cocked her head to the side for a moment. "You know, no we don't. But that's a brilliant idea. I'm ashamed I never thought of it myself." Grabbing a portfolio off of the front desk, she flipped it open and glanced at whatever was inside. "If you're free this afternoon, I could have someone escort you around."

"That would be great."

"Around three o'clock? In the main salon?"

Elle had easily agreed. Even if she'd had something else planned—and she didn't—she'd have changed it.

So, here she was, standing in the center of the silent main salon. Alone. Waiting for whoever would appear. She was restless, a mixture of anticipation and expectation bouncing through her body. She tried not to show it, but wasn't sure she succeeded.

Zane walked in, pushing an extra shot of energy into her already buzzing system. It was like giving espresso to someone who'd already been drinking coffee all day.

Instantaneous overload.

Her mouth went dry. Her sex grew wet. And an insistent ache began to throb between her thighs.

Damn, she did not need this right now. She didn't want it, this awareness and desire for the man.

Zane moved farther into the room. Elle scooted behind one of the chairs, conveniently putting it and a brightly polished mahogany table between them.

He hadn't spoken, and she suddenly felt the need to

fill the empty space. "I'm meeting Marcy. She's going to show me the resort's art collection."

"Wrong. I'm going to show you the art collection."

"You?" Elle tried not to let her surprise color her words. "Why you?"

"Because she asked me to."

"Don't you have better things to do? Other guests to accost?"

He chuckled, the low rumbling sound rolling through her tummy and tickling her already sensitive nerves. "Probably. But I promised to keep an eye on *you*. In any case, aside from Simon, I know the collection best."

Now, that puzzled her. She wondered if Zane's knowledge of the resort's art collection had to do with personal preference or his job.

"Why?"

"I told you. Because Marcy asked me."

"No, why do you know the collection so well."

"I had to inventory it for insurance and security purposes. When I got here, Simon had works of art worth hundreds of thousands of dollars hanging in the front hallway. No alarms. No protective glass. Hell, he barely knew the real value of what he owned. He'd bought pieces when he liked them, caring little for their value."

Or their provenance apparently, but Elle wasn't going to be the one to bring that up.

"So you swooped in and saved the day?"

He frowned. She didn't care.

"No. I did what he needed me to do. I identified the pieces that had greatest value and implemented a security protocol. Learned a few things while I was at it."

"Bully for you."

"I could do without the sarcasm."

"I could do without living inside a fishbowl."

All day, she'd felt his eyes on her. At the pool, she'd wondered if he could see her in her bikini. And whether he preferred that to the soaking-wet dress she'd worn last night. Or the casually comfortable shorts and shirt she'd thrown on this morning. As she'd chatted up a couple of women inside the restaurant at lunch, she'd wondered if he was listening to their conversation.

All day, the man had haunted her every thought. Her every move.

And here he was again. Only, this time, he was flesh and blood and not some phantom that floated over her shoulder.

Which begged the question, could she keep her hands to herself? She certainly hoped so. She had no desire to end up back in those cuffs…or maybe she did.

5

"Art, huh? How'd that happen?"

Zane stood next to Elle, his arms crossed over his chest and watched. Something was wrong. While she gave every appearance of being engrossed with the pieces they were seeing, her body was strung tighter than the electric guitar Simon no longer played but refused to get rid of. Zane's gut told him something else was going on here, but he wasn't sure what.

When Marcy had told him she planned to take Elle on a tour of the art, alarm bells had begun to ring through his head. Marcy had been so excited about the potential for setting up the tour for other guests that she hadn't really stopped long enough to consider the security implications. But then, it was his job to protect the resort and the people who lived on and visited Île du Coeur.

He'd chastised her for not telling him sooner and then immediately cast himself as tour guide. He might not know anything about the pieces, but he could fake his way through.

At least Elle hadn't questioned him yet.

But then, he wasn't sure she was really paying attention to anything he said anyway. Which sorta bugged him.

However, he had the perfect opportunity to dig a little deeper and he wasn't going to waste it.

"What? Oh, it started when I was three and painted a beautiful—" a small smile touched her lips and made something inside his chest tighten "—what I thought was a beautiful butterfly on the den wall with my finger paints."

She turned to him, looking him in the eye for the first time since he'd entered the salon. "The rest was history. It's just part of who I am. I see something— pretty, scary, upsetting, anything—and I want to capture that moment on paper or canvas or clay or whatever I can get my hands on. Other people keep their memories in their head—" she turned back to the painting "—I keep them all around me so I can touch them whenever I need to."

Whether she'd meant to or not, she'd just given him a wide view into her psyche. He could see the girl she'd been, surrounded by scraps of paper and paint— smeared cardboard, the good and bad things accessible so that she could process them however she needed to. She was probably saner than the rest of the world because she'd figured out the best way to deal with the inevitable pain, fear and unhappiness.

He sure as hell hadn't figured it out.

Clenching his fists, Zane pulled himself back into the moment. This was not about getting to know this woman. It wasn't about finding things about her that he could like. It was about learning why she was really here so he could prevent her from hurting the people around him.

"Did you study or are you self-taught?"

They moved slowly into the next room, an echoing ballroom. The space was cavernous and empty. A shiver snaked down his spine. There was something about the loneliness of the place that gave him the heebie-jeebies. It seemed like the perfect spot for a sad ghost to hang out. Hell, considering the history of the place, there probably was one. He could almost see an old woman, dressed in her finest ball gown, twirling in the center of the room. Alone.

As a cocoa plantation, Île du Coeur had a rich and difficult past. Slavery was part of life back then, and that meant unhappiness and fights for personal freedoms. There were many gruesome stories of inhumane owners, but equally uplifting stories of triumph over adversity. Gentility had been the outward face, but the underbelly tended to be ugly.

There were stories of lovers and quarrels and things that had likely been embellished over the years. Hell, there was even a local legend that said visitors to the island would find their heart's desire…even if it wasn't what they'd expected. That was how the island had gotten its name. And while he didn't believe in that kind of stuff, he couldn't help but watch Elle and wonder what she'd come to the island searching for.

Weak sunlight filtered through a wall of windows and French doors that led out to balconies. At strategic intervals between the old-fashioned wall sconces hung several works of art. Escape didn't tend to host weddings or large receptions, so this room was rarely used.

Walking around to an alcove, Zane flipped several switches and flooded the space with light. Three crystal chandeliers swayed softly above their heads. They were original to the building, and expensive as hell.

He heard her quick intake of breath as she walked unhurriedly into the center of the room.

"It's beautiful."

"Yep."

"Why wasn't this in the brochure? This would be an amazing place for a wedding. It just feels like it holds so much history." She spun around, slowly taking in the room with eyes that missed nothing. "I can imagine the balls that must have once been held here."

"Next on Marcy's list. She has big plans for special-events marketing. Assuming Simon agrees."

Elle turned toward him, taking several steps closer. "Why wouldn't he?"

Ah, the million-dollar question. "Why does Simon do anything? Or not do anything? No one really understands what goes on inside that cluttered and scary place Simon calls a brain."

She laughed. The sound was rich and...real. It was real. After hearing so many women walk around the resort tittering and giggling and faking their way through, it was unexpected to find someone who was so comfortable in her own skin that she had no artifice.

Elle Monroe was who she was and she made no attempt to hide that or change or gloss over even the things about herself that weren't perfect.

It was...attractive.

"Anyway, I'm a little bit of both."

"What? Both of what?" He stared at her, slack-jawed, trying to figure out what the heck she was talking about.

"Schooled and self-taught. I went to the Savannah College of Art and Design. But before I got there, I had years of experience to fall back on. I took classes in high school. I spent hours in my own head and room, learning through trial and error. So, both. And I think I needed both."

"I know what you mean. You can run mock drills and go through all sorts of training, but until you're on the street with a criminal who was a gun pointed at your head, you just don't know. It isn't the same until it's real."

She nodded. "Exactly."

"So, are you successful?"

"So, why aren't you an agent anymore?"

He raised a single eyebrow, they both knew he wasn't going to answer that question. It was too complicated. It dredged up issues he wasn't ready to deal with. And he wasn't here to share with her. He was here to interrogate her. And he wasn't doing such a great job of that.

"I support myself with my art, if that's what you're asking. I just finished a gallery showing and sold most of my pieces. It's taken a while, but I'm building a name for myself."

She wandered off across the room, her footsteps echoing hollowly. "At first, it was difficult. My father and brothers gave me hell on a regular basis, kept telling me I needed to live in the real world and get a real job."

Elle stopped in front of a painting, one that had been sold with the property. Simon hadn't been motivated to replace it, content to use what was already here. Less work. It was appropriate for the space, the scene of a Victorian-era ball, with glittering women and dashing men.

He didn't think Elle was actually seeing the painting, though—it was unremarkable in just about every way. But her eyes darted back and forth across the canvas and her forehead was furrowed as if the scene held the secret to world peace.

"I know they were just worried about me. I couldn't afford an expensive apartment and settled for one in an area of town that had a reputation. But I refused their help. And I refused to move back to my dad's. I needed to live on my own, to support myself."

"To show them you could do it."

Her eyes were sparkling as she glanced over her shoulder toward him. He felt as if he'd just received a gold star from his favorite teacher.

"I'm surprised you understand. I would have expected you to agree with them."

"Well, apparently you're successful enough to afford a vacation at this place, so it's easier now. I probably would have agreed with them then."

Her lips twisted in a grimace telling him she didn't like his answer.

Something snapped between them. Understanding. Attraction. Connection. A sizzle of energy he hadn't felt in a very, very long time. It was seductive and scary.

After Felicity's death, he'd pushed everyone away. It was easier than dealing with their pity and sadness. He had enough issues of his own to contend with, he couldn't handle everyone else's, too.

But it was lonely, this solitary confinement he'd condemned himself to. At first, he hadn't minded living in his own head. Simon was here if he'd really needed someone. Although, their relationship had never really been like that. They would do anything for each other, but they didn't get too deep into the important things.

Elle intrigued him. And he didn't want that. He didn't want to be pulled into anyone's orbit—especially that of a woman who might be a criminal. He'd tangled with enough criminals, and Felicity had been the one to pay the price. While Elle didn't strike him as the kind of person to hurt someone…he wasn't sure he trusted his instincts anymore.

He found himself stepping closer to her anyway. Dust motes swirled between them in the weak sunlight that filtered deeper into the room. Her eyes widened, the pupils dilating, pushing out the gray for a black circle that dragged him in.

Her lips parted and her breath sighed across them, waiting. He reached for her. He couldn't have stopped himself even if he'd tried. He should have walked away. But all he could think of was kissing her until they were both numb, senseless with desire.

The scent of her, a mixture of sunscreen and tropical flowers, slammed into his chest. The tempting tip of her pink tongue darted across her lips, leaving them gleaming. His arm wrapped around her back, arching her into his body. There was no easing into the moment. He wasn't gentle. He wasn't careful. But then, neither was she.

His lips crushed hers. His palm buried in the hair at the nape of her neck, forcing her into an angle that brought them tighter together. The strands of her hair slipped through his fingers, soft and silky, even as their tongues, teeth and lips dueled against the strength of an attraction neither of them wanted.

Warring emotions—hunger, misgiving and blind greed shot through him as her teeth nipped at his bottom lip. He growled deep in his throat. Somehow they made it across the room. In the back of his brain, he heard the reverberation of her back hitting the wall, the rattle of paintings and sconces jarred for the first time in years.

She'd whipped him into a frenzy with little more than her lips.

Her fingers dug into his back, raking down his skin even through his shirt. His hands raced over her, trying to experience everything all at once. One of her legs found its way up over his hip. She used her heel to press into him and urge him tighter against her. The welcoming warmth of her body awakened feelings and sensations he hadn't experienced in way too long.

A purr of satisfaction vibrated through her as he dragged his lips down the column of her throat. It tickled and awoke in him a need to taste her entire body, to touch and lick every inch of her before he starved to death.

A loud bang echoed through the room. Instincts kicking in, Zane spun on his heel. Gunshot. No, it couldn't be. It hadn't sounded quite right. But, he couldn't afford to take that chance. They were out in the open, completely vulnerable with nothing to hide behind, nothing for protection. Tugging her wrist, he pulled her as close to the ground as possible.

"Stay low," he hissed at her as he scanned the room. It was empty. Nothing moved.

Behind him, Elle ignored his order. With a snarl, he whipped his head around to her and said, "Stay down!"

It took him a few seconds to realize that she held something in her hand. For a brief moment, he wondered if she was the threat.

With a twist to her lips, she let the object go. It dropped to the polished wood floor with a loud crack. The thud echoed off the walls, making it sound as if it was coming from all different directions.

The thing bounced up once and then rocked before

settling on its side. A sandal. A teeny tiny sandal with a large wooden wedge heel.

Her shoe had fallen off her foot in their melee.

Laughter fizzed inside him. It was better than giving in to the embarrassment.

With a sheepish grin, he pushed up from his crouch on the floor and shrugged. What else could he do?

Admit that shoe had just saved him from making a huge mistake? Not likely. At least, not to her face. He might be rusty, but he wasn't suicidal.

With a stilted laugh, Zane said, "We hope you've enjoyed the Île du Coeur art tour. If you'll see Marcy on your way out, I'm certain she has some questionnaire so you can evaluate my performance as tour guide. And if she doesn't, I'm sure she'll make one up."

Elle's eyes clouded at his words. "Wait. What?"

"Tour's over."

She gave a quick shake of her head, as if trying to bring everything back into focus. He understood the urge. He was trying to make the two alternate universes before him merge together—the one where they were back against the wall, finishing what they'd started, and the one where he kept his distance from the woman who was far more than she said she was. He needed to get away from her. Now. Before he did something stupid.

"This can't be it."

"Oh, it can be."

Her eyes narrowed. "There has to be more art."

"Why do you say that?" And with such conviction. She hadn't asked a question. It was a statement.

How did she know there was more art?

Slowly, he answered, "There are more pieces in the private areas, but you can't see them. Hence the word *private*." Hoping to figure out what she was fishing for, he didn't give her any details.

She sputtered. Zane moved into her personal space again. His reception wasn't nearly as gratifying this time as it had been before. Instead of melting into him, she stiffened, as if he was about to attack her.

"What are you after, Elle? Tell me. Maybe I can help you."

She pushed against his chest, heat the only thing in her eyes now, although they were still dilated with the dregs of passion. Apparently, he wasn't the only one regretting their encounter.

"If you know what's good for you, Officer, you'll stay away from me."

He pushed closer. He told himself it was intimidation, but he was lying. Even as her warmth caressed his skin, a deep breath dragged the scent of her back into his body.

He was a masochist. That was the only explanation.

"Why would I want to do that?"

"Because your precious video camera now has evidence that you assaulted me." She gestured with her chin toward the corner of the room and the eye of the camera staring back at them.

His lips curved into a sneering smile. He had to give her points for ingenuity and effort.

Leaning down, he brushed his lips against her ear and whispered, "We both know that's a lie. That camera will show two people caught up in the passion of the moment. You can lie to yourself all you want, but those cameras never do. You wanted me to touch you, Elle."

He pushed away, his neck bent over her and his lips dangerously close to hers. His brain was fighting with his libido when she did him a favor.

Reaching out with the flat of her hand, she slapped it across his face.

"Let's see what your cameras say now," she said over her shoulder as she stalked out.

Zane cupped his cheek. It stung, but wasn't nearly the worst pain he'd experienced at the hands of a woman.

SHE FUMED. HER HAND THROBBED where she'd hit his rock-solid jaw. But she didn't want to visit the onsite doctor. She'd have to explain, and that was something she refused to do. Mostly because she had no idea what had really happened.

One minute they'd been practically tearing each other's clothes off, the next Zane had been back to the demanding hard-ass with the glint in his eye and smooth-talking words that rocked her to the core.

Because he'd been right.

If her shoe hadn't fallen off, who knew what they'd be doing right now? No, that wasn't true. They'd have been having sex. In the middle of a public place. And she wouldn't have given a damn.

What was wrong with her?

A shiver racked her body at the thought. Damn the man. He was demanding and egotistical and difficult and passionate. She knew to the depths of her soul that if he ever did touch her again—if she let him touch her again—she'd be consumed by him.

He was an overachiever who put everything he was into whatever he did. The same intensity that drove her insane outside of the bedroom would no doubt be mind-blowing inside it. He'd be the kind of lover who would leave her a puddle of mindless goo. The way he looked at her, as if he knew every inch of her body and what to do with it... Heat began to pool in the center of her sex. She ignored it. Or tried to.

Wasn't going to happen. That slap should protect her from herself.

She'd lived with men who exhibited that same intensity her entire life. The drive her father put into his job. The way he'd brought every case home with him, even if he hadn't meant to. The way he'd gone to extremes to protect her from the sickening world he saw everyday. The way he'd expected perfection from her—and everyone else around him.

She couldn't live up to the expectations. She wasn't perfect. No one was. Not him, not her brothers. Not Zane.

And she had no doubt that he was cut from the same cloth, would require perfection from himself and beat himself up when he couldn't deliver on such an impossible standard. She didn't need that sort of upheaval in her life.

Right now, things were practically perfect. She made a decent living doing what she loved. She had freedom. No one she had to share her space or herself with. It was easier that way. Less messy. Less demanding.

Damn it. Why couldn't she convince herself she wasn't interested in him? Never, in her entire life, had she become so entangled with a man in such a short space of time. Had it only been yesterday morning when she'd been handcuffed to a chair inside that tiny room? It really had. And already Zane was occupying every spare second of her mind.

She needed a distraction before she did something very stupid and very regrettable.

Pulling out the folder that the front desk had given her upon checking in, Elle stared down at the turquoise paper and the list of activities that were scheduled for the week. She hadn't bothered to look at it before, because she'd fully intended to be otherwise occupied. However, she really needed a distraction right now.

Well, there was a bonfire on the beach in about an hour. It might be…interesting. Definitely a diversion, if nothing else. And maybe if she was lucky, Zane wouldn't be there. Because if he was… Balmy night, sparkling stars, flickering fire, tropical setting—it would be too easy to give in to the chemistry between them.

He wouldn't be there. He'd been working all day. Had been forced to give her the tour of the plantation— and she knew without being told that art was nowhere close to his hobby. While he'd stood patiently as she'd studied each piece, she could feel the tension that had coiled through his body.

If she had been anyone else, she probably wouldn't have noticed. But while half of her brain had been studying art, the other half had been zeroed in on him. She couldn't help but be aware of him. The scent of him, the heat of him, how he'd come close and then backed away. She'd wanted him to brush up against her just so she could feel his skin on hers for a second.

And then she'd realized how childish the thought was. She'd never been shy about sex before in her life. Whenever she'd wanted a man, she'd told him so. If he was interested, they got naked. If he wasn't, she moved on to someone who was. It wasn't difficult and it wasn't complicated. She hadn't played these kinds of games in years, didn't have the time or patience for them.

Elle wondered if things were different—if she wasn't planning on *recovering* something from his employer— would she have jumped Zane by now? Possibly. Hell, probably. But things weren't different. They were complicated and she didn't do complicated. She did quick, easy and painless.

And something told her nothing about getting involved with Zane would be painless. He was complicated and moody and closed off and uptight and... everything she shouldn't want and apparently did.

So she'd go to the bonfire. Maybe the romantic setting would spark something with one of the other single men on the island. Maybe an anonymous fling with someone who wasn't trying to wheedle his way into her brain and get her to admit to committing a crime would be just what she needed.

And maybe pigs would fly.

6

ZANE WATCHED FROM THE shadows. He could join the lively group of people clustered around the large fire the ground staff had laid and lit, but he wouldn't.

The minute he'd seen Elle on the screen, exiting her room, he'd jumped out of his chair to follow her. The black-and-white picture hadn't done her outfit justice, fading the vibrant colors and muting their impact.

She wore a sarong skirt in a wild print of reds, golds, blues and greens. It wasn't long and flowing like he was used to, but cropped shorter, about two inches above her knee. The slit at the front played peekaboo with whatever she was wearing beneath. And for the safety of the men around her, he hoped it was a chastity belt because he couldn't trust his reaction if one of them attempted to touch what he desperately wanted but couldn't have.

It was an optical illusion meant to play with a man's mind. The top of the opening halfway up her thighs never crept high enough to reveal anything. But each time the motion of her scissoring legs stretched the fabric and teased against that slit, he held his breath, hoping it would go higher and praying that it wouldn't.

She had some flowy top on that he didn't pay much attention to other than to notice it was solid red. He supposed she'd call it something like crimson or magenta or some other fancy word for plain old red. Chunky jewelry ringed her neck and right wrist, some big stones in beige and brown polished to a shine.

Her flat sandals slapped against the pavement of the path. There wasn't much to them, either, just thin leather straps that connected to the sole and wrapped repeatedly around her foot and up the lower part of her calf. His mind immediately flashed to a vision of her naked, those leather thongs crisscrossed down her palms and wrists, tying her to his bed.

Damn. Not at all professional.

It had taken him a few minutes to realize that she'd dressed deliberately. For the past two days, she hadn't put much effort into looking sexy. Most of the time he took it for granted that their guests had come to the island for one thing and one thing only. Privacy and the opportunity for a romantic setting and hot steamy tropical nights. That's what they specialized in.

After that first night, he'd assumed Elle had other things on her agenda. Hell, he knew it.

Tonight, though, she was apparently joining the ranks of the hedonists.

Jealousy and a protective, possessive bent he didn't like twisted deep inside. Zane frowned. It had never concerned him before that their female guests regularly went into rooms with strangers and closed the doors so no one else could see. They'd never once had an incident. They didn't run extensive background checks on their guests—not like the one his friend was running on Elle. But they did some basic searches, knew none of their guests had criminal records or were wanted by their respective authorities.

The thought of Elle disappearing behind some closed door with a horny stranger made his fingers clench into fists and his teeth grind.

And maybe that was why he currently stood in the shadows of the trees that edged the beach. Or maybe it was just his training finally overruling his hormones. Either way, he watched as Elle laughed and flirted, drank and talked. She was beautiful, not that she hadn't been every other time he'd seen her. Even soaking wet, her hair bedraggled and dripping, the woman had been breathtaking. Fiery. That was what it was. She attacked everything in her life full force, no excuses, no apologies, no equivocations.

It was unusual. Refreshing. He'd come from a life that was nothing but lies. He'd had to keep the truth from Felicity for months about what he really did when they'd first started dating. Once he'd told her, he'd had to keep the nature of his assignments a secret. And while he hadn't outright lied to her about them, he hadn't exactly told her the truth, either. The CIA operated on a need-to-know basis, and she hadn't qualified.

What would it be like to be able to say every damn thought that popped into his head?

Terrifying. Some things were meant to be private. Elle didn't seem to see the world that way.

Elle settled by the fire on one of the logs the crew had set out. Some couples crowded closer to the bonfire, jostling each other to get marshmallows on sticks into the flames. Heckling burst through the air as someone's gooey treat caught fire and charred an unappetizing black before falling into the flames with a sizzling plop.

The guy she'd been talking with stood up, walked across to the bar set up several feet away and returned with two drinks. He handed her another one of those frothy pink concoctions she'd been drinking last night. She sipped and smiled before the guy sat back down. As far as Zane was concerned, he looked smarmy. A businessman trying very hard not to look like one. He'd shed the suit Zane instinctively knew he lived in when he was at home. But the closest he could get to relaxing was a pair of khaki shorts, a crease ironed down the side that he knew the man hadn't put there himself, and a dark green Izod shirt. The gold-and-diamond watch on the yuppie's wrist had to cost five thousand dollars, easy.

And his loafers were clearly Italian leather. Who wore Italian leather to the beach?

This guy was not the type he'd expected Elle to go for. There was a bad boy across the fire pit who kept eyeing her. He was shirtless, with a tattoo covering one shoulder, worn jeans and a light in his eye that said he knew how to live life to the fullest. Now, that was who he'd expected Elle to go for—someone dangerous and just as daring as she was.

Although, he was glad that so far she had ignored bad boy's pointed looks of interest.

Zane scooted closer to Elle and the yuppie. He wasn't spying… He was doing reconnaissance. There was a difference.

"Do you have any plans for tomorrow? I was thinking about the ballroom classes. I've always wanted to learn the tango." Even the guy's voice sounded false, his laughter too forced.

"Hmm." Elle sipped at her drink, a smile curving her lips. "I'm actually planning on going out into the jungle to paint. Marcy, the director, managed to get me some paints and canvas from the mainland. They aren't mine, but they'll do in a pinch."

"Aren't you supposed to be on vacation?"

"Sure, but I should have known I'd want to paint when I saw the beauty of the island in that magazine ad."

"You saw it, too? That's the reason I came here. It looked so…perfect."

Elle laughed, the low-throated sound jolting through Zane. "Exactly."

"So do you know where you're going to paint? Maybe I can come with you. Watch. I've always wanted to watch an artist at work."

God, what a terrible line. If the guy knew anything about art, Zane would eat the bullets out of the gun currently locked in the safe back in his bungalow. Zane might not know much, but at least he didn't pretend an enthusiasm he hadn't felt until Elle had stormed into his life.

"Sorry, no. No one sees my stuff until it's done. Personal rule of mine."

"Oh." If Zane's teeth hadn't been squeezed together so tightly, he might have smiled at the crushed expression on the other man's face.

"I heard one of the staff talking to a couple about a waterfall back a little ways into the jungle. I might end up there. Or I might end up somewhere else. I think I'll just start walking and see where the path leads me."

Elle went to take another sip of her drink, only to find that the glass was empty. With one of those tinkling laughs, she gave the guy an almost sheepish grin. "Looks like I need another drink. It was very nice to meet you, Stewart."

Zane found himself lifting a single eyebrow in the dark where no one could see it. The brush-off. And not a very subtle one. Elle pushed up from the log and sauntered across the gathering, toward the bar. Stewie frowned, but then followed her back into the fray. Zane watched as he shifted his focus to another woman and began chatting. This one looked a little more receptive to his advances, not that Zane cared if Stew ended up with company tonight.

Dismissing him out of hand, Zane turned his attention back to Elle. Her back was against the bar, one hand holding a fresh drink and the other arm stretched out across the wooden lip of the counter. Her knee was bent, one sandal pressed tight against the side of the bar.

Her eyes ran across the crowd. From his vantage point on the other side of the clearing, hidden by the shadows, Zane couldn't tell if she was searching for someone in particular or just looking.

He considered going to her, but before he could move, bad boy was beside her.

Elle smiled up at the guy. Zane couldn't see her eyes clearly enough to tell whether the smile was real. A few seconds later, when Elle shifted her body closer to the man, Zane realized it didn't matter.

He watched as Elle stood on tiptoe, arched her body away from the bar and into the man's space. She lifted her chin, moving closer so that he could lean down and whisper something into her ear.

She laughed. The sound didn't make it to Zane, caught by the wall of ambient noise from the other people between them, but he saw. She pressed her palm against his chest—his bare chest. Zane half expected her to push the man away; instead, she seemed to use his body to steady her own off-balance posture.

Dropping back down onto her heels, Elle took a step away from him. Setting her half-empty glass onto the bar behind her, she turned to leave, throwing a quick glance back at the man as she walked away.

The man stood there for several seconds, watching her go. He turned to speak to several people he'd been talking to earlier, and ninety seconds later, bad boy was following her.

And Zane was following them both.

ELLE WALKED THROUGH THE silent halls. Everyone was either out on the beach or at the bar or holed up inside one of the rooms, enjoying the sensual setting and tropical heat.

She was heading back to her room. Alone.

There was no question she could have had a companion…if she'd been interested in anyone but Zane occupying her bed.

All night, she'd felt his eyes on her. How many times had she scanned the people around her, looking for him? She could feel him, caressing her skin as he'd watched. Or maybe that was just her overheated imagination.

He couldn't have been watching through the lens of a damn camera. Not out in the open on the beach. No place to hang one from, right? Although, it did make her wonder what the range of those things was. Something she'd gone her entire life without needing to know.

Even now, she could swear she was being followed.

Elle stopped and whipped her head around, staring down the empty hallway and feeling like an idiot.

Definitely her overactive imagination. Knowing that

Zane and his staff were watching apparently made her jumpy.

Still, she couldn't stop her feet from moving just a little faster as she turned the corner. Her room was the last one on the right, across from the freight elevator masquerading as another room door.

A sound echoed down the hallway she'd just come from. Elle's heart rate picked up and her body flushed warm with unease. Hadn't that hallway just been deserted?

She was five feet from her door, fumbling inside the clutch she'd brought to find the key that suddenly seemed to have disappeared. Throwing glances over her shoulder, she let out a tiny groan as the guy she'd been talking to at the party rounded the corner behind her.

His eyes immediately found her, standing alone and vulnerable at the end of the hallway. Or at least she assumed he thought she was vulnerable. He was far enough away that if she could find the damn key, she could slip into her room and avoid a confrontation.

She might know how to protect herself, but the first rule her father had taught her was "fight only if you have to." Exhaust all other options first.

A small spurt of relief flooded through her as her fingers closed around the cold edge of the key. The guy—the one with the tattoos, tanned muscles and "God's gift to women" chip on his shoulder—had taken only a few steps when all hell broke loose.

One minute he was striding down the hallway, the next he was slammed against the wall, Zane's arm lodged firmly against his throat.

The key slid through Elle's fingers, dropping to her feet with a metallic ping as she sped toward the two men.

"Why were you following her?"

"Zane, what are you doing? Stop it!"

He threw a glance her way before dismissing her, but the quick glimpse she got showed eyes that were glittering chips of glass, refracting the light and reflecting the anger rolling around inside him. His jaw was tight, the muscles in the arm pressed underneath the other man's jaw pulsed with the intensity of the hold Zane had—on the other man and on himself.

"I asked you a question."

"I wasn't following her, man." The words scraped past Zane's hold, making Elle cringe. They sounded painful.

She reached for Zane's arm, hoping that she could pull him back. The muscles beneath her hand rippled, but he didn't budge.

"Zane, let him go."

The other man slowly moved his arm, reaching into his pocket to pull out a key identical to her own. "My room's right over there." With a trembling finger, he pointed down the hallway.

Zane raised his arm from across the other man's neck. Holding both his hands up in a nonthreatening gesture that really meant nothing at this point, he took two steps away, giving the man just enough space to scoot around him toward the door he'd indicated.

Elle almost felt sorry for him as he sent several furtive glances over his shoulder. Up until the moment his back was pressed against the wall and an elbow was cutting off his circulation, Elle would have said he was bad straight down to his toes. Now she wondered if the tattoos were fake and the long shaggy hair was a wig. The guy had squealed like a little girl.

She supposed Escape was the sort of place where

someone could alter their persona. Become the person they'd always wanted to be.

As the man slid his key into the lock, his hand only slightly shaky, she wondered what he did in real life. Accountant. Insurance actuary. Something very boring and safe. He could have made money as an actor, at least until someone rammed him up against a wall.

"Are you o—" Zane took several steps toward her but he never made it where he wanted to go. Instead, Elle struck out at him, grasping his arm and spinning his body, pinning him face-first against the wall.

She wasn't stupid. She knew that if she hadn't had the element of surprise on her side, she never could have gotten the jump on him. Even now, if he'd really wanted to, he could have gotten out of her hold. But he might have hurt her in the process and she knew enough about Zane by now to realize he'd never in a million years let that happen.

Hadn't he just defended her? A woman he suspected of lying, stealing and the worst sort of treachery?

He'd never hurt a woman. He was a protector. Well... okay, unless she was a danger to others. And they both knew Elle wasn't.

"What the hell..." His words, even muffled against the wall, sounded lazy and unconcerned. Was he laughing at her?

"I can take care of myself, Officer Zane."

"Special agent. How many times do I have to tell you?"

She shrugged, hoisting his arm just a little higher with the motion. His body moved with her, sliding against her own.

Bad miscalculation.

How could she go from indignant to aroused in the space of a single heartbeat?

"I get it. You can take care of yourself. That doesn't mean you might not need protection now and again."

"From the staid accountant taking a walk on the wild side?"

"Have you ever met a serial killer?"

Zane flexed his wrist beneath her hold, testing her. At least, she thought that's what he was doing, although it also had the added advantage—or disadvantage, depending—of forcing the flat of his fingertips to brush against the underside of her breast.

She breathed out the single word, trying to stay focused. "No."

"Most of them are psychopaths pretending to be staid accountants and boring lawyers."

Elle wanted to take a step back, but if she did that she would have lost the advantage of her weight pinning him against the wall. She had no doubt that, at the first sign of weakness, he'd have their positions flipped, her own body pressed tight to the wall. Again. Not something she wanted to repeat. Okay, not something her brain wanted a repeat of. Her tingling, aching body could just stuff it.

Gritting her teeth, Elle ignored the growing sensations. "Probably why they're serial killers. Boredom can drive you to any number of things."

Taking advantage of the inch of space she'd inadvertently given him, he rolled his hips beneath hers. The movement pressed the tight muscles of his ass against the cradle of her hips. Her thighs spread wider, crushing back down against him. Her vacant hand grasped on to his hip, hoping to hold him still with the combination.

"Tsk, tsk, tsk."

Her fingers brushed against something cold and hard tucked into the waistband of his pants. Her gaze darted to the side, eyeing the smooth plastic surface of his all-access key card.

She didn't think. Pushing up on tiptoe, Elle pressed her body closer. She enjoyed the way he tensed beneath her, the way his breath caught in his lungs for a second before bursting out on a groan. He watched her with narrowed, glittering eyes. Not even his vulnerable position, his cheek pressed against the wall, could diminish the intensity and appreciation in his appraisal.

She was torturing him, distracting him, but she was also torturing herself.

And if she was going to, why not take whatever she could get?

Pressing her lips to the side of his neck, she placed an openmouthed kiss there. Sucking his flesh into her mouth, she kept the pressure up until she knew he'd wear her mark tomorrow.

She slid the key card into her own waistband, then reached around them both once her hand was empty again.

And she filled it with him instead. She wasn't surprised to feel the length of his erection straining against the cotton of his pants. She relished it. Reveled in it. Enjoyed the fact that he was man enough to let her hold him here and enjoy being at her mercy.

His breath whistled out between clenched teeth as she squeezed. Her hips rocked against his—no design, but rather an unavoidable reaction—as her palm stroked down the hard length of him.

This time, she was the one to close her eyes, lost in the pleasure of touching him.

She might have gone further—might not have been coherent enough to stop herself—if a squawk hadn't split the cocoon of silence around them.

"Zane. Come in, Zane. Do you need backup?"

The voice coming from his other hip startled Elle enough that she stepped back, letting him go.

Slowly he turned, his body never losing contact with the wall. His eyes, shuttered and dangerous, flashed at her. The golds and greens and browns intrigued her, the colors more pronounced now than she'd ever seen them.

Without a word, he reached for the phone—the kind that doubled as a two-way radio—held it toward his mouth, pressed a button and said, "This better be good, Tom."

"Well, s-sir…" The voice stammered out of the radio, followed by a squeal that had them both cringing and Zane pulling the thing away from his head.

"I'm sorry. I was scanning the monitors and saw you and her…" The words trailed off into silence as Zane slowly turned his head, staring straight into the eye of a camera she hadn't noticed until right now.

Even from here, Elle had no doubt the man on the other end of that radio could see the promise of retribution as clearly as she could.

She should thank the man, whoever he was.

Taking the opportunity of Zane's distraction, Elle slowly moved backward, one small step after another. By the time Zane returned his focus to her, she was ten feet away from him, her key retrieved from the floor where she'd dropped it. She watched him surge from the wall, a spurt of adrenaline and unbridled passion shooting through her.

He stalked toward her, an aroused animal on the hunt

for his prey. He was all muscle and sinew and the promise of pleasure she couldn't imagine. A shiver snaked down her spine.

She couldn't stick around long enough for him to catch her.

Yanking open her door, Elle didn't even bother to look back at him before saying, "Night, Officer Zane," and slamming it in his face.

Her back pressed against the door, Elle's chest rose and fell. Her eyes closed as she sagged against the wood. She could hear the sound of him standing on the other side. Or maybe that was her imagination. Was the door thin enough that she could really hear him?

She almost jumped when she heard the soft thwack of his palm against the wood behind her. But the blow hadn't been in anger. In fact, it hadn't been forceful at all.

But it did make her realize something. What if he decided to follow her into the room? Surely he had some way to access all of the guest rooms. Though the key card wouldn't work on them, the hotel must have a few copies of each key for housekeeping and emergencies.

She wasn't scared because he might break some moral code to follow her inside. She knew to the depths of her soul that the first time she said no, Zane would back away and leave her alone.

But they both knew she had no desire to say no.

Her problem would come when he reached for that key card and realized it was missing.

Pulling it out of her waistband, Elle flipped the card over to stare at the laminated side of the identification. Edwards. That was his last name. And for the first time Elle realized she'd come close to having sex—not once but twice—with a man when she hadn't even known his full name. What did that say about her? Nothing good.

Zane's stern likeness stared back at her. Surprise, surprise, he wasn't smiling. But then, she couldn't remember ever actually seeing the man smile. Smirk maybe, but really smile so that it lit up his eyes? She racked her brain and came up empty. Although she supposed they hadn't exactly experienced any moments together that engendered laughter.

Guilt swamped her as she continued to stare at the pilfered card. What had she done?

Once again she'd gone off half-cocked. It wouldn't take him long to realize his card was gone and start wondering if she'd taken it.

The moment her fingers had touched it, she'd realized the innocuous piece of plastic was her all-access pass to the private rooms that he'd told her about this afternoon.

The problem was, the second she used the card, he'd know it. In one of her earlier career choices—one that hadn't lasted—she'd worked for a bank. The key cards they'd used for restricted areas had been coded so that security could keep tabs on access and higher-ups could monitor who came in late and left early.

Zane would have no less.

Damn it. Now what was she going to do?

She had the Holy Grail, the thing that she needed to move one step closer to finding her grandmother's painting, and she couldn't use it.

Not without getting caught.

Not without Zane realizing she'd stolen it from him.

And for some reason, she really didn't want him to learn that his low opinion of her was justified.

So she'd have to return it without him noticing, and hope that he assumed he'd misplaced it.

With a groan, Elle covered her face with her hands. The key card dangled accusingly between her fingers as she slid down onto the floor. Pressing her forehead to her knees, she wondered if she'd ever learn to think before she leaped.

With a sigh, she acknowledged probably not. If she hadn't learned the lesson by now, there was little hope that she ever would.

However, she promised herself that this was her very last foray into theft—of any kind.

She'd have to find another way to get her grandmother's painting back.

7

ELLE WAS UP BEFORE DAWN again. She told herself it was because she wanted to head out and catch the early light. It was really because guilt had kept her up and she'd finally decided distracting herself with work was better than lying in bed mentally yelling at herself. That accomplished nothing.

With narrowed eyes she stared at the easel Marcy had managed to find and decided it was just too big to haul into the jungle. The island wasn't that large, so she probably wouldn't be going far, but she didn't want to get the bulky easel stuck somewhere and have to abandon it. Instead, she threw the paints, brushes, sketch pad and the smallest canvas Marcy had found into the duffel she'd carried onto the plane.

Grabbing bottled water, pastries and a few pieces of fruit from the cold breakfast bar, she headed out. The path to the waterfall wasn't paved like the rest of the resort, but it was fairly easy to follow. Apparently she wasn't the only guest who'd ever ventured out onto the wild side of the island for a little adventure.

The vegetation closed around her, swallowing her

up into a world of towering trees, climbing vines and tropical flowers. The first thing she noticed was the lush colors—intense greens, vibrant blues, pinks that popped and reds so deep the flowers looked as if they were bleeding. Sunlight, bright and clear streamed down through the canopy in stripes of gold, gilding the already brilliant surroundings.

The next thing she noticed was the sounds—birds and insects and chattering animals she couldn't see buzzed, screeched and called to each other. It wasn't still, and yet a sense of peace descended around her. She wasn't alone, not really, but she felt as if she might be the only person on the island.

Her muscles warmed with the exertion of walking and the heat of the sun as it climbed higher into the pale blue sky. Stopping to pull a bottle from her pack, Elle dragged half of it down. And realized that another sound had joined the cacophony around her. It had probably come on gradually which was why she hadn't noticed at first.

Rushing water.

Gathering her pack, Elle headed down the path at a sprint, eager to see what the jungle hid.

She broke through the trees to find a beautiful little oasis. It was breathtaking.

The water was crystal clear, only about three feet deep in the eddying pool. She could see all the way to the silt bottom that stirred beneath the currents. To her left, a small curtain of water fell over the jagged edge of rocks about twenty feet in the air. There were more rocks at the bottom. A ring, set around the bubbling water as it rejoined the pool at the base. The wall of water danced on its way down, shimmering and parting and closing again. She could tell there was a small cave behind the falls, but couldn't see how far back it went. A small stream exited to the right, flowing back into the jungle.

Maybe later she'd explore the cave. But right now, her palms itched to have a paintbrush against them.

Tearing into her pack, Elle dropped to the ground right where she stood and grabbed for the canvas.

First, she sketched the picture she wanted to capture, frantically dragging a pencil across the rough surface in an attempt to grasp the ancient mystery of the place. Despite the sunlight, it had a dark knowledge, as if it had stood here forever, watching as humans and other creatures passed through its shadow. Remembering, but not judging.

She lost track of time. Not an unusual occurrence when she was engrossed in a project. The food she'd brought was completely forgotten. Even the water, despite the increasing heat as the height of the sun peaked above her, lay untouched inside her bag.

It wasn't long before the paints followed the sketch, overlaying the crude charcoal markings with layers of vivid color that only barely seemed to match reality as far as she was concerned.

Her legs were cramped from sitting in one place. She stared at the canvas and the explosion of lines and arcs and colors that she'd pulled together to form the picture before her. She wasn't happy. Something was missing, but she couldn't figure out what.

That was the most frustrating part of her art. She looked up at the untouched world before her, and back down at the canvas balanced on her knees. They were identical. At least to her eye. And still it wasn't right.

With a groan of frustration, Elle reached into the

bag, took out everything that was inside and gingerly laid the wet canvas down onto the collapsed bag.

She'd eat something. Cool off in the water, explore the cave. Get some distance and then come back.

Maybe then she'd realize what was missing.

"WHERE IS SHE?"

Zane walked into the Crow's Nest without bothering to say good morning to Tom. He was later than normal. Typically he would have relieved Tom around eight, but several things had delayed him. A call from his buddy at the CIA. The background check on Elle had revealed nothing earth-shattering. She'd been a rebellious teenager with a single sealed record and no run-ins with the law since.

She'd filed a report when her apartment had been broken into several years ago. The officer who'd been assigned the case had noted her insistence that an ex-boyfriend had been responsible. The officer had never found any evidence—or the ex-boyfriend—to corroborate her theory. That wasn't to say he hadn't been responsible. Elle seemed to have a habit of choosing the wrong men.

The sealed record had involved a boyfriend, an older one, and several friends who'd apparently broken into the school gym. They hadn't done any damage, so the judge had given her and her friends community service. The boy, however, had an outstanding warrant for dealing drugs. Thanks to their little stunt, the man had ended up in prison for six months. A nasty fellow who had continued down the wrong path and was now behind bars for the third time. And set to stay there for the next ten years. The world was better off with him locked up.

But at least Elle seemed to have learned from the experience. Aside from her bad taste in men.

He'd also had a meeting with Simon and Marcy, which Simon had delayed for an hour. If he hadn't been jittery himself, he might have enjoyed watching the steam pour out of Marcy's ears. As it was, by the time Simon had called them into his sanctuary, Zane hadn't exactly been smiling, either.

It was after ten and God only knew what kind of trouble Elle had managed to find for herself in the past several hours.

"Gone."

"What do you mean, 'gone'?"

Tom shrugged. "She left around six, duffel bag slung over her back, and headed out into the jungle."

"And you didn't stop her?" Zane growled.

"Why would I? People go to the waterfall all the time."

"Couples go to the waterfall. Tell me someone else was with her." Part of him hoped she'd taken that damn yuppie along, not that he'd be able to save her from a poisonous snake or a broken ankle when she fell off a path, but surely the man could run for help. Part of him dreaded the idea of her heading off into the dense vegetation with someone else. Someone who wasn't him.

"Nope, she went alone."

"Goddamn it." Zane slammed his hand against the frame of the door, not caring that the room seemed to shake around him. Of course she'd gone out there alone. Idiot.

And he hadn't told her not to. He'd meant to. Last night. But he'd been distracted by that moron following her, and then by her dominatrix routine and the sleight of hand that she thought she'd pulled on him.

Oh, he'd been perfectly aware the moment she pulled that key card out of his waistband. She was good, but he'd been trained by the CIA.

He'd let her take it, wanted to see what she would do with it. The minute she swiped that card through any of the doors, he'd know it—and hopefully learn exactly why she was here. What she was searching for.

He'd checked the log before he'd left his house this morning. He knew she hadn't used it. And now he knew why. She wasn't even on resort property.

"You stay here. You're running the Nest today," Zane growled.

"But I've been on all night."

"And you'll be on all day. Maybe next time you won't let someone wander into the jungle alone." Turning around, he was halfway down the corridor when he picked up his two-way and yelled into it, "And tell Marcy where I'm going!"

Elle was hours ahead of him, but at least he had a decent idea of where she'd gone. At a steady walk, it would take him about a half hour to get to the waterfall. If he'd been in the city, it would have taken him about twenty minutes—it was only about two miles away. But the path wasn't straight, and the going was rough and crude in several places, winding back on itself to avoid sharp drop-offs that the dense trees and bushes hid.

Fear had him moving faster. A vision of Elle lying at the bottom of one of those drops, her body broken and bloody leaped into his brain. The vision was quickly overlaid with the memory of Felicity as he'd seen her from their apartment window, dead on the sidewalk below.

He'd been too late to save her. He wouldn't let that happen to Elle. He couldn't lose her, too.

Zane burst into the clearing just in time to watch Elle pull her T-shirt over her head and drop it onto the mossy ground at her feet. With a flick of her ankle, her shorts joined the pile. Her skin glowed beneath the sun, a damp sheen from the heat making the tanned surface glimmer.

She wore nothing but a pale pink bra and a matching pair of boy shorts.

The underwear covered just as much as—if not more than—most of what passed for bathing suits by their female guests. But somehow, what Elle wore was far sexier. Maybe it was the forbidden element. She hadn't intended anyone to see her strip down to her bra and panties and plunge headfirst into the shallow pool.

The anger and fear that had dogged him the entire sprint here was now mixed with all-consuming lust. The mixture was dangerous…deadly.

Without thought, he charged after her.

"What the hell do you think you're doing?"

Startled, Elle spun, spraying water around her. Droplets clung in her hair, diamonds against the fiery red.

"What are you doing here?" Surprise was soon replaced with lazy calculation. Her eyes narrowed and she stared at him for several seconds before she fell over onto her back. Her hands played languidly across the surface as she floated in the water.

Her bra was soaked, the pale pink turning almost transparent as her breasts jutted up out of the water. He could just see the darker circles of her areolae and the peaks of her tightened nipples.

"I told you I'd be watching." His voice sounded gravelly, even to his own ears, filled with craving and crusted with the last dregs of his fear.

She shook her head. "You're wasting your time."

Zane shrugged his shoulders. They both knew that was a lie, but he wasn't ready to tip his hand about the key card, so he said nothing.

Matching her conversational tone, he walked closer to the bank. Toeing off one shoe and then the other, he left them on the path. "Are you stupid or just suicidal?"

"Neither," she said, lifting her head out of the water long enough to shoot him a taunting grin.

"You have to be one or the other to walk into the jungle alone, without telling anyone where you were going."

"You managed to find me."

"Luck."

A smile played across her lips. "Don't sell yourself short, Officer Edwards."

"Special agent."

Her smile grew.

He waded into the water. She flicked her feet and moved farther away. Grabbing the hem of his shirt, he tugged it over his head and flung it onto the sandy bank.

He'd stopped long enough to put on some shorts before heading out to the waterfall. He didn't bother taking them off, and surged into the water after her. This time, he was the one with the element of surprise.

He grasped her ankle, towing her back through the water toward him. She thrashed. His eyes closed to protect himself from the flying wall of water that washed over him. She rolled like a gator, flinging her free foot and twisting his arms. He didn't lose his grip.

"Let me go."

"Not a chance."

With his free hand, he reached down for her, intent on dragging her out and giving her a solid piece of his mind. Somewhere between intent and execution, it went completely awry.

He'd meant to grab her arm. Instead, he got a palm full of silk-covered breast as she squirmed in the water.

She stilled. His body loomed over her and she stared up at him.

The clear water did nothing to cover her body. It only amplified what he'd been dying to get a glimpse of for the past few days.

She was beautiful. Perfect. And her nipple peaked beneath his palm, pricking his conscience and urging him on all at once.

He tried to move back, but her body arched into his hold, following the warmth of his hand.

Her face was blank, but her eyes burned as she watched him. They'd both been fighting this. He'd tried to make it go away, but it wouldn't. In fact, it was only getting stronger. Each time he saw her, he wanted her more. And considering he'd done nothing but watch her since she got here, he'd definitely been playing with fire. Zane reached for her. She didn't move away, she didn't come closer. She stood there, the muscles in her chest expanding and contracting on her labored breaths. His own lungs felt starved for oxygen. No, starved for her.

Burying his hands into the hair at her nape, he pulled her to him and took what he wanted.

And she let him. Her body arched back in his arms, giving him better access to her mouth. Her arms hung limp at her sides. But he could taste her desire, could feel the heat of it coming off her skin in waves, mingling together just as their mouths and tongues collided.

He scooped her up into his arms. The walk to the beach was endless and immediately forgotten as soon as he laid her out on the ground close to the forest floor. Fallen palm fronds, soft wildflowers and spongy moss that seemed to grow only close to the water cushioned the ground and provided the perfect bed.

He followed her down, rolling onto his side so he could look at her. She stared back, the passion-soaked haze gone from her eyes. Her lips pulled down into a frown as she said, "We probably shouldn't be doing this."

"Nope." She was right. There were so many reasons he should keep his hands off her—forefront in his mind was that he really didn't think he could trust her. And considering he had enough trouble trusting people these days... But his body wouldn't seem to listen. So here they were, together, in a secluded clearing on a private tropical island. And he wasn't going to be the one to stop the inevitable.

He reached for her, his hands skimming across the smooth plane of her stomach, as his lips tasted the curve of her shoulder. She was sweet and slightly salty from her hours under the sun. The tropical floral scent he'd assumed was artificial seemed to be embedded deep within her skin, quintessentially Elle and definitely not from some bottle. It was exotic, just as she was, and reminded him of steamy, moon-soaked nights. Nights he wanted to spend with her.

Zane watched as her eyes closed in bliss. As sexual caresses went, he would have put both low on the scale for what might have caused her pleasure. But the reality was stamped across her face.

He moved his mouth closer, trailing kisses across her collarbone to the sensitive curve of her neck.

"Just so we're both clear," she breathed out, before rolling beneath his hand to grab for him.

Her fingers dug into his skin, pulling him closer to her body. What she was saying was hard to miss, and still he had to ask.

"You're sure about this?"

Rearing up on her elbow, Elle looked down at him. She was fierce and beautiful and full of life. Her skin glowed with energy, not just some sprayed-on tan but the vitality of a life lived to the fullest. Her silvery eyes flashed at him, a reflection of the need pulsing through his own body. A half smile tugged at the corners of her lips, timeless and mysterious. As if she knew things he'd never understand. Had experienced things she'd never share with him.

Although, he hadn't really asked her to. He had plenty of secrets and a history of his own. Things he couldn't share. Memories he wouldn't let taint this moment.

Elle was here, and right now he didn't want to be anywhere else.

"Shut up and kiss me," she whispered.

8

ELLE WATCHED THE PLAY of emotions as they crossed Zane's face. If he had any idea of the glimpse into his mind that he'd just given her, she was sure he would have bolted back to the safety of his hidey-hole, the resort.

She didn't know his story, but she could guess. And in the grand scheme of things, it really didn't matter. She didn't need to know him in order to enjoy the physical explosion he could tease from her body.

She wondered just how many women Officer Edwards had been with since he'd come to this place. She was absolutely certain she wasn't the first guest to have been attracted to the resident cop. Lots of women fell for that man-in-uniform, save-the-world, Superman complex that he hid beneath his stern outer shell.

She wasn't one of them. Wouldn't be one of them.

Pushing up onto her knees, Elle reached behind her and snapped open the catch of her bra. She let it glide down the length of her arms to fall into a wet puddle across his body. She enjoyed the hiss that leaked through his teeth, wondering if it was because the cloth had been cold and wet, or because he liked what she'd revealed.

Without waiting to find out, she rose to her feet. The boy shorts she'd put on this morning were by far the least sexy underwear she owned. At least, she thought so. But the look in Zane's eyes told her maybe she needed to reevaluate. Certainly, they were less than cooperative as she tried to peel the clinging material from her wet skin. Somehow, what she'd meant to be enticing was quickly turning into a moment of embarrassment when they rolled into an uncooperative ball of cloth just as she tried to get them over her hips.

That is, until his hands swept hers away. She looked up from her struggle to find Zane on his knees at her feet. She had a brief moment to think, *I could get used to this,* before his hands settled on her body and coherent thought fled.

With gentle tugs, he worked the soggy material down her legs, cupping one ankle to steady her when she lifted a foot so he could toss the panties aside.

His hands grasped the globes of her ass, pulling her closer toward him. His mouth touched down on her stomach, his tongue dipping to swirl into her belly button. A tug of something deep inside followed the rush of slick need between her thighs.

Her eyes closed and her hands found a steady perch to hold on to when they landed on his shoulders. His breath tickled her body. His hands wandered, sweeping across her breasts, tweaking her nipples, sending chills up and down her spine. But she couldn't concentrate on that. Not when the moist heat of his mouth was so close to the aching source of her desire.

His mouth brushed against the curls covering her

sex. She wanted him to spread her open, to touch her and put them both out of their misery.

Instead, he asked her a question that had her groaning with disbelief, even as the words reverberated inside her.

"I don't suppose you have a condom in your bag of tricks over there."

"Why would I have a condom?" she gasped. "I'm on the Pill."

"Not the same."

Pulling out of his hold, she said, "Are you saying you think I'm going to give you something?"

"No, I'm saying we don't know each other."

With a groan, she collapsed onto the ground beside him, knowing that he was right. Neither of them had come into the jungle expecting to jump the other's bones.

"Damn it." Her words held none of the frustration she actually felt.

"My sentiments exactly. Although…" With a feral smile that had another spurt of desire rushing through her, Zane dropped to all fours and crawled his way toward her. "I'm sure we can think of something to do…to tide us over until we can get back to the resort."

Elle's eyes narrowed. There were two things that her brain snatched from the statement he'd just made. One, he had every intention of continuing what they'd just started once they got back to the resort. This wasn't a one-off moment-of-opportunity kind of thing. Apparently, it was more like the vacation fling that everyone seemed to think she'd come to the resort for in the first place.

She flipped that around in her brain for a minute and

realized she was perfectly fine with that. She wasn't sure once with Zane Edwards would be enough anyway.

Two, he didn't intend to leave her aching and aroused in the middle of the jungle.

That she could also live with. In fact, she wasn't sure she'd be *able* to live if he didn't finish what they'd started—one way or another.

Her legs had sprawled at odd angles when she'd fallen to a heap in frustration. She didn't bother to move them now. She'd never been one of those women who was embarrassed to let a man see her naked. She was confident enough in her body and her sexuality. Besides, she made a point of never stripping in front of a man if she didn't know one-hundred percent that he wanted to sleep with her. She figured once they were to that point, it really didn't matter if she had a few extra bumps and lumps—although she didn't, at least not yet.

Zane prowled between her open thighs, grasping a leg to pull it up so he could run his lips down the inside of her thigh.

She let him mold her, moving her where he wanted, because she trusted that whatever he did would feel fantastic.

And she wasn't wrong.

His mouth closed over the weeping center of her sex. Her body bucked at the contact, the electric current of pleasure driving her hips off the ground and her flesh tighter against his mouth.

His tongue flicked across her clit. Back and forth in a maddening rhythm that just wasn't enough. He teased and tortured her, she couldn't have said for how long. She was mindless with need, her body drawn so tight she was ready to snap.

And still, he wouldn't let her come. He'd take her

right to the edge and then back off, blowing across her skin in a frustrating caress until she dropped away from the edge again.

She whimpered, a sound she was absolutely certain she'd never made in her life. And then she begged. Incoherent words that she hoped he couldn't decipher, but knew to the core of her being he understood.

At one point, she reached for him, trying to pull him up her body so that she could touch him, feel him, drive his erection into her and end her misery.

He wouldn't let her.

Instead, he distracted her, anchoring his mouth back over her clit and driving a finger deep inside her. It was too much and she was too close. Her body did exactly what he wanted it to, exploding around him as the band of arousal he'd wound so expertly finally snapped.

The world faded away, even the bright sunlight behind her closed eyelids going black. She couldn't breathe. She couldn't think. All she could do was feel the pleasure as wave after wave of it washed over her.

Seconds, minutes, hours. She didn't know how long it took for her brain to begin working again. Probably not as long as she thought, though, since both of them lay on the ground, their chests heaving in unison.

"Holy shit."

He chuckled, a sound that had strain running all through it.

Rolling onto her side, Elle propped her head on her hand and watched him. His eyes were closed, his jaw tight with the effort of just lying there. His hands were fisted at his sides, handfuls of earth oozing through his fingers.

And his erection strained against the damp cloth of the shorts he still wore.

Her mouth watered.

She wanted to see him, feel him, know him.

Leaning down, Elle brushed her mouth across the side of his neck, enjoying the way his pulse leaped beneath her lips. When she was close to his ear, she whispered, "My turn."

His body pulsed beneath her. Really, that was the only word she could think of to describe it. She could feel the desire he was holding back surfing just beneath his skin. It was a living, breathing thing. And they were both slaves to it.

Brushing her palms down his chest, she went to work on his waistband. The button popped easily, but the waterlogged zipper didn't want to move. She was about to give up when he said, "Get it down or I'm going to rip it apart. That'll be hard to explain when we get back." His words were guttural, telling her just how close to the edge he really was. She had no doubt at all that he meant what he said. Having her touch him was more important at that moment than anything else—including having to explain an embarrassing situation.

Power surged through her. He wanted her that much. With renewed conviction, she wrestled the stubborn zipper open, tugging the teeth apart.

He wore nothing beneath. Elle wondered if that was standard operating procedure for this man and then thought it probably was. If he'd been thinking of sex, he would have had a condom.

His erection sprang free, the throbbing length slippery with his desire.

"I'm sorry, it won't take much," he pushed out between clenched teeth as he watched her watching him.

She ran a single finger down the length of him, relishing the way he jumped into her touch, wanting more.

"Damn, Zane, who asked you to be Superman? I didn't. Do you think it bothers me that you drove me insane and managed to barely hold it together yourself? You just gave me the best orgasm of my life. I really don't care if it takes you three seconds or three hours, as long as you enjoy what I'm about to do to you."

She dipped toward him. Her hair fell around her face. The ends feathered across his skin, making his stomach muscles contract.

She ran the flat edge of her tongue along the entire length of his erection, enjoying the way he breathed out "sweet lor—" before his voice dropped off into an incoherent gurgle when she opened her mouth and took him deep inside.

He was big, filling her mouth in a way that made her internal muscles clench. What she'd give to feel him moving inside her. Later. Soon.

For now, she contented herself with the texture of him beneath her tongue. He tasted of salt and man. Smelled of musk and sex. He was hard and soft all at once, silk-covered steel.

She sucked. He writhed beneath her, grasping the back of her head and urging her nearer.

She teased him, using the wet heat of her mouth to get him close, before backing away and leaving him restless. His eyes promised retribution, a payment in kind that she would relish.

"Witch," he breathed as he reached for her, pulling her up and crushing her mouth with his own. His large palm engulfed her smaller hand, guiding her until her fingers were wrapped tight around his shaft. "Finish me," he said. The words were supposed to be an order from the calm, capable, unflappable Officer Edwards.

But Elle heard the desperation beneath them. Remembered begging him for her own release minutes before.

She was nicer. She wouldn't make him beg.

Watching as ecstasy suffused his face was almost as amazing as feeling him pulse and explode beneath her fingers. His body strained against the whipcord of pleasure as it pounded through him. His fingers clenched against her body, one hand buried deep in her hair, the other anchored securely on her hip. His hold might have hurt, if she'd noticed. But she was focused solely on him, on the moment his guard was completely down, and she could see behind the mask to the man beneath.

He collapsed to the ground, dragging her with him.

Sunlight streamed across her body. Lazy warmth stole through her. And her limbs suddenly seemed weighted down, too heavy to move. Her eyelids, too.

She let it all go, falling asleep in his arms. Something she hadn't let herself do in a very long time.

"YOUR SKIN'S GOING TO burn." Zane's deep voice called her back to the land of the living. His fingers played across her skin, making random patterns.

Without opening her eyes, she smiled and said, "I don't burn. My Nana was Italian. I have Mediterranean blood running through my veins."

His fingertips brushed over the ends of her hair, "So where did the red come from?"

"Nice 'n Easy?"

His other hand strayed to the curls at the juncture of her thighs, calling her a liar without saying a word.

The smile on her face spread. "My Irish grandpa." She cracked her eyes open, twisting her head so she could look up into his face. "Lucky it wasn't reversed, huh? Pasty skin and curly black hair probably wouldn't have been so pretty."

"Pretty? Yes. You? No. Somehow that kind of ice-princess beauty just wouldn't have suited you. You're…"

"A pain in the ass?"

"*Explosive* was what I was actually thinking, but yeah, *pain in the ass* works, too."

She reached behind her and grabbed the first thing her hand landed on, her discarded bra, and lobbed it at him.

Scrambling away, he scooped up his damp shorts and put them back on. Snapping them up as he walked away.

But he didn't get far. He stopped next to the bag that held all of her stuff.

He stared down at her unfinished painting and Elle tried desperately not to squirm. She wanted to bolt up and snatch it away, but something inside stopped her.

"Now, this is beautiful," he said, glancing back at her over his shoulder.

"It isn't finished."

"Looks perfect to me," he said, reaching down as if to follow the lines with his fingertip.

"What do you know?" Pushing to her feet in one motion, she walked toward him, swatting his hand away from the still-wet canvas before he could smudge it. "No touching."

His arm snaked around her waist, pulling her tight into his body. "I hope you don't really mean that," he growled against her neck. The rumble of his words echoed through her body, igniting the embers of the fire their love play hadn't truly extinguished.

She'd come. Rather forcefully, if she was honest.

Satisfaction should be rolling through her right now, along with the need for a longer nap.

Instead, her blood hummed just beneath her skin. She wanted him again. Right now. In the sand, on the rocks, in the grass. Wet, dry, she didn't care. Elle hadn't had enough of Zane Edwards.

And that scared the shit out of her.

He was the kind of man she always stayed away from. Always with a capital *A*. He was controlling, overbearing and demanding. Honorable, beautiful, the type who put everyone else's safety way before his own. He was guilt ridden—about what, she didn't know, but she recognized the signs well enough. She'd lived with men who blamed themselves for so many things beyond their control.

She'd lived all of her life beneath the thumb of that kind of man—men. And while her father and brothers loved her, it hadn't been easy. The experience had taken a toll on all of them, and she had no desire to set herself up for a relationship that would drain her the same way.

Not that Officer Edwards was offering her anything other than a vacation fling. She was jumping way ahead of the situation. But the problem was that she knew herself well enough to recognize the signs. Bad signs.

In a few short days, he'd worked his way under her skin, like a splinter. She didn't want to, but she cared about him. Bad, bad idea. They were wrong for each other. She was here only for a little while and he distrusted her every move.

Yeah, not a great foundation for anything.

Not that they *had* anything.

Zane's hands wandered down her body, a welcome distraction from the thoughts racing around her brain.

He molded her against him, arching her spine. His mouth found the now-speeding pulse at the curve of her neck and sucked, making it leap higher. Heavy heat pooled in the center of her belly.

And suddenly her concerns didn't seem so important. Besides, this was a fling. In a few days, she'd be gone—hopefully with her grandmother's painting—and Zane and his guilt-inducing demons would be left behind on this tropical paradise. Nothing but a pleasant memory....

What harm was there in taking a few more helpings of what she'd already had? The milk had already been spilt, after all. Might as well enjoy the milkshake—with whipped topping and sprinkles—while she had it. She could worry about the consequences later.

Besides, her body responded to him, whether her brain wanted her to or not. She wasn't about to start something again that neither of them had the supplies to finish, however. The next time they got down and dirty, she wanted the whole damn deal. She wanted to feel him inside her, long, hot and hard. Nothing else would fulfill the need already building within her.

"Oh, no, you don't." As difficult as it was, Elle wedge a hand between them and pushed him away. "Unless you know how to fashion a condom out of palm fronds—and if you do, I'm going to kill you for not doing it sooner—we're going to hit Pause until we get back to the resort."

His lips frowned at her but his eyes smoldered, heavy with promise and passion.

"I do need to get back," he grumbled. "I'm cooling off first, though. Wanna join me?"

The corners of his mouth twitched. If she hadn't been looking at it longingly, she probably would have missed the microscopic tell. And wouldn't have paired it with the twinkle of mischief that had entered those heavy-lidded eyes.

"No way, mister." She took two steps away. If she got in that water with him, it would be another hour before they went anywhere.

"Suit yourself." Not looking back, he waded out into the softly churning water.

Elle watched for several seconds as he skimmed beneath the surface, toward the waterfall. He broke free directly beside it and stepped into the tumbling sheet of water, letting it wash over his body. His eyes were closed, his head thrown back—it was the first time she'd seen him without the usual intensity slightly pinching his face.

He looked relaxed. Blissful.

Without thought, Elle sank onto the sand, reached for her canvas and began painting.

It took her barely any time at all to add Zane to the picture. His features were blurry, making it look as if you were viewing him through the curtain of water. No one would be able to tell that the man in the picture was Zane.

But she'd know.

Looking down at it, tightness began to gather in the center of her chest.

He was what had been missing.

9

ZANE WATCHED ELLE WALK away. The farther she got, the more anxious he felt.

The woman was a ticking time bomb. She was impulsive and reckless. Trouble followed her wherever she went.

But that wasn't the only reason his skin suddenly seemed too tight for his body.

He was fighting dueling urges—to haul her back to him and to run as fast and hard as he could in the opposite direction.

He didn't know which one to follow.

Oh, he knew which one was intelligent. Elle Monroe was trouble. He didn't trust her...unless he could see her, at least. But therein lay the problem. She was like the sun. The closer he got, the stronger the pull of her orbit became.

He didn't want to get sucked in. Couldn't afford to get sucked in, to care. But he also couldn't seem to rid himself of this crazy urge to protect her—from everyone and everything, but mostly from herself.

And sleeping with her hadn't made it any easier. In

fact, it had only made the problem worse. It was like giving a starving man bread and then throwing him back into the desert before he could finish the loaf. He hadn't realized what he'd been missing until it was dangled in front of his face.

To ask him to turn away from Elle now that he'd had a taste…that was just torture.

If he was smart, he'd avoid her for the rest of her vacation. He wouldn't compound one mistake with another.

But then, he'd never claimed to be smart. Arousal still buzzed through his system, skimming just beneath the surface. Despite the fact that they'd both climaxed, neither one of them had been fulfilled.

He knew it wasn't a good idea, but he wanted more. For the first time in a very long time, he realized he was going to step over the line into the gray areas. Before Felicity's death, those gray areas had been his familiar hunting grounds. He'd been more than willing to bend the rules, manipulate them to get the result he wanted— bad guys off the streets. Her death had changed everything.

But apparently he hadn't changed enough.

Two days ago, he would have bet his entire salary that Elle Monroe was a thief just waiting for the perfect opportunity to rob them blind.

Part of him didn't want to believe what his brain was telling him. He'd seen her with his own eyes, breaking and entering. But she hadn't actually stolen anything. At least, not that night.

He knew for a fact that she was currently in possession of his key card, but so far, she hadn't gone anywhere with it.

She didn't have a record. Not one that mattered. Was

that because she wasn't a criminal or because she just hadn't gotten caught? That, he had a hard time believing... He'd caught her twice and he was rusty as hell.

Something didn't add up. Whatever was going on, he couldn't trust her.

But somehow, his dick wasn't getting the memo.

Zane stepped into the air-conditioned lobby of the main building, sighing in relief from the tropical heat. His forward momentum stopped dead though when his boss's slow Southern drawl melted across the lobby. "There you are. Everyone's been looking for you. For hours... Apparently, you were stupid enough to storm into the jungle alone and not answer your cell phone when Marcy called repeatedly."

Shit. Simon might be lounging against the front desk, his back pressed into the wood and his arms draped over the top, but the relaxed pose was a complete lie. The hard glitter in his eyes showed his true feelings.

"I told Tom where I was going."

"Yes, but apparently when you didn't return immediately with the troublemaking redhead in tow, he got concerned that she'd murdered you and was burying the body."

"Elle is a lot of things, but murderer isn't one of them."

Simon's gold-blond eyebrow arched, "Well, isn't that an about-face from two days ago, when you thought she could possibly be the devil incarnate."

Zane scrunched his forehead into a frown. "I don't think I ever said that."

"Not in so many words, but the handcuffs said it for you."

Zane kept his mouth shut. There was nothing he

could say. At least, nothing that might help. Simon might appear to be a lazy playboy, but behind that easygoing facade was a brain that worked at lightning speed.

"Why don't we go upstairs and talk?"

That was the last thing Zane wanted right now. "I need to relieve Tom. Besides, I'd hate to interrupt your work."

"Oh, don't worry, you've already done that. And Tom is fine. Don't think I don't know he owes you for that little fling of his a couple of weeks ago."

Damn, the man was observant. Simon noticed everything. Even Zane often forgot just how deep those skills went.

"Fine. Lead the way."

The men traveled through the resort, to the back elevators. Simon's quarters could be reached only through the private employee sections. In fact, the main elevators didn't even have a button for the fifth floor. Most of the guests didn't realize it existed.

They rode up in a charged silence. Whatever their "meeting" was about, Zane knew he wasn't going to like it.

As they entered into his private domain, Simon didn't even stop at the living area out front. It was usually where Simon held his conversations with employees. Despite the fact that they were friends, Zane had seen the back rooms only a handful of times. Simon just preferred to keep them off-limits. Which was how Zane knew he'd really stepped in it this time. Simon strode straight on through to the office at the back. And closed the door behind them.

The view out the windows was amazing. Bright blue sky stretching into clear turquoise water. Golden sand, lush green trees. He could just glimpse the pool complex, but the angle of the windows and the landscaping blocked most of the activity. From Simon's office, he could almost believe the island was deserted except for the two of them.

He was certain it was one reason Simon spent so much time up here. Well, that and he was busy.

Simon plopped into a huge black executive chair. The mechanism squeaked gently as he leaned back into the worn leather.

There wasn't another chair opposite the desk as most executives had. Again, Zane knew this was no oversight but a deliberate attempt to convince whomever did manage to get inside the sanctuary to keep their visit as short and painless as possible. He guessed it was most often Marcy. And he had no doubt she ignored Simon's blatant rudeness.

Zane also chose to ignore Simon's psychological warfare and plopped down onto the corner of an overstuffed sofa that sat along the far wall.

Almost before Zane's butt had connected with the cushions, Simon waded straight in. "I'm worried about you."

Zane took a moment to settle his body, using the delay to gather his thoughts. "Why?"

"Don't play innocent with me. I've known you for too long. Tom told me about your little episodes with the redhead. And then you disappear into the jungle with her for hours at a time."

"That's a complete misrepresentation of what happened."

Simon waved away Zane's protest. "Semantics. We both know nothing innocent happened in that jungle.

First, you were gone too long. Second, your clothes are all rumpled and slightly damp."

"It's hot out there, man."

Simon leveled a laser stare at him, daring him to continue pushing the story they both knew was a lie.

This was where working for your friend got a little screwy. Up to this point, he and Simon hadn't had a problem at all. Sometimes, it didn't pay for your employer to know you too well.

"Look, since when do you have a problem with guest fraternization?"

"Since I'm worried it might interfere with your ability to do your job."

Now, that pissed him off. Never mind that he was just lecturing himself about the same issue. It was one thing for Zane to remind himself of his priorities. It was entirely another for Simon to question them.

"Fuck you. I've busted my ass for you over the past eighteen months. I've given you no reason to question my ability and commitment."

"I don't question your ability. Or commitment. I question whether you can evaluate this woman objectively anymore. I know you. And I know what happens on my island. You haven't slept with a woman since you got here and I'm guessing since Felicity died. If you didn't screw the redhead in the jungle, you'll probably do it the next time you see her."

Zane opened his mouth to protest, but closed it again because he couldn't.

"I've seen the tapes, Zane. You practically devoured each other in the middle of the ballroom."

Zane's molars began to grind. Simon wasn't bringing up anything he hadn't already thought... It just sounded worse when it came from his friend and boss.

"Look, I don't care if you feel like screwing every bimbo who walks through the door. And if that's what it'll take for you to get over Felicity, I'll start lining them up myself. But you're on dangerous ground with the redhead, man. As your friend, I thought I should tell you. As your boss, I have to say that if your personal relationship with her leads to a problem, I'm going to have to fire you."

Zane stared at him. What else could he do? He hadn't needed the reminder. He knew what was at stake. The problem was, his dick thought the price—whatever it turned out to be—was worth paying.

Simon leaned into his chair, slowly rocking it back and forth, the squeak of the mechanism grating in the charged silence that had settled over them.

"So, you wanna give me details. What's she like?"

Zane's entire body stiffened. They were a long way from their days of being frat brothers, sharing everything—including women on occasion.

An overwhelming wave of possessiveness washed over him as he shot up from the sofa. "What the hell, Simon." It took him several seconds to register the glint of mischief sparkling deep in those damn blue eyes.

"Bastard," he mumbled as he walked toward the door. He didn't care if Simon was done with him. He was done with Simon.

ELLE HAD GONE TO ANOTHER one of the single's mixers the resort specialized in. It was better than sitting alone in her hotel room, her mind racing with thoughts she didn't know what to do with. This party was themed... togas, if you could believe it. And she, apparently, had been the only one reluctant to relive that college experience. Everyone else had been having a ball. She was all for cutting loose, but it was ridiculous. Perhaps she would have enjoyed it better if she'd been drunk, but after her up-close introduction to the pool, she'd tried to limit the pink drinks.

She had no idea where Zane was. What he was doing. When she might see him again. If she might see him again.

Elle didn't often battle insecurity, but it was certainly rearing its ugly head at the moment. The feeling was far from pleasant.

Her life might be full of chaos—artistic bursts of inspiration, unwashed dishes piled in the sink and papers falling off the hall table. But when it came to relationships, she kept things simple. Easy. Uncomplicated.

There was nothing about her relationship—for lack of a better word—with Zane that was easy or uncomplicated. It had *turmoil* written all over it. Hell, they could barely come together without some kind of argument or misunderstanding.

And that damn key card was always in the back of her mind. If he found out she had it, that would only reinforce his low opinion of her. She really didn't want that to happen. She didn't want to see disappointment fill those multicolored eyes.

She'd seen that enough growing up with her father. She'd worked hard not to experience the kind of guilt that emotion could cause.

She'd give the key card back. It was that simple. She just needed to figure out how. Then maybe if she was lucky, she'd spend the rest of her vacation with the sexy head of security. She'd have to find another way to recover Nana's painting. Only God knew what that was. She was completely out of ideas.

Melancholy settled over her as she rode the elevator up to her floor. Halfway down the hall, she glanced behind her just to make sure she really was alone.

She looked up into the face of the security camera mounted in the corner of the hallway and thought briefly about doing something naughty, but decided she couldn't be certain Zane was actually the one behind the bank of monitors. And, frankly, she'd embarrassed herself enough with the security staff over the past several days.

All night, she'd looked out for him, hoping he'd appear in the crowd of sheet-draped drunks to sweep her away from the juvenile chaos. He hadn't appeared. Nor had the sensation of being watched returned.

She'd gotten so used to the constant itching at the back of her neck that she'd reached up to rub the spot several times before she'd realized it was gone. Had been ever since she and Zane returned from the jungle.

Elle fought back the rising tide of disappointment as she pushed into her room.

And nearly screamed when a man rose from the chair in the dark corner.

"I've been waiting for you."

His body was in shadow, the drawn curtains blocking out the bright Caribbean moonlight. The only light in the room spilled from the hallway. It barely touched where he stood, leaving his face completely indecipherable.

But she could see his eyes, sharp and bright. They cut through the gloom, the intensity and desire burning there sending a wave of goose bumps across her skin.

She let the door slam behind her, plunging them into total darkness. It was sensory deprivation of the most delicious kind. She could hear the rustling of his clothes as he moved across the room. The rasp of denim, the soft shuffle against hardwood.

Even before he touched her, the scent of him drifted out to caress her skin. She gulped in large pulls of air, drawing him even closer. Tonight, overlaying his normal masculine musk and sex smell, she detected something tropical. Not flowery or fruity...lush and very manly, possibly left over from their foray into the jungle. Memories ripped through her body, bringing a heat and need that nearly drove her to her knees with the intensity. She wanted to burrow her face into his neck. She wanted to pull him so close that nothing could stand between them. She wanted to taste and touch and absorb him into every pore.

But she couldn't find him.

She reached out into the dark, a blind woman searching for a touchstone but not finding one.

Something sounded to her right and her head whipped toward it. "Zane?" she whispered. She had no idea why, other than the inky darkness seemed to demand it. A quiet reverence. A prayer that he hadn't been a figment of her over-stimulated imagination.

He didn't answer.

Her body jerked in surprise when his mouth touched down onto her shoulder. Languid heat spread through her body, weighting her limbs. She'd worn a strapless top, a band of elastic holding the blue-and-green fabric as it flowed away from her body and skimmed just to her hips. She'd paired it with some white capris, enjoying how it made her newly tanned skin glow.

Apparently, she'd made the right choice. Her body melted against his solid frame. She fought the urge to just give in and crumple beneath him, offering anything and everything he wanted. But that wasn't her. She didn't give in that easily.

Instead, she chastised him. "You weren't there tonight."

"I was there. You just couldn't see me." His words and lips brushed against her skin as they traveled over the ridge of her collarbone and across to her other shoulder.

"Liar. I would have felt you. Even when you were watching through the cameras, I knew when you were there."

He trailed warm kisses down the length of her arm, stopping at her elbow to let his tongue swirl there for a moment before continuing down to her wrist. Goose bumps erupted across her skin. The sensation was unexpected. She'd never thought of her elbow, hand and wrist as particularly sexy. And surely not erogenous. But warm heat flooded her body and she felt the urge to squirm beneath his caresses.

Her palm curled, her already sensitive fingertips rubbing against his stubble-roughened jaw. Maybe it was the lack of vision, but her senses seemed on high alert. Waiting. Anticipating his next touch.

But that wasn't really her. She wasn't the waiting sort.

Using his hold on her wrist as an anchor in the dark, Elle turned until her body was behind his. Her breasts pressed against his back, tingling and puckering with their demand for a more direct stroke. He kept hold of one arm, making it almost completely useless.

With the other, she wrenched the tails of his shirt free from the jeans he wore. Her palm surfed across the valleys and peaks of his well-defined abs. This thirty-something man had certainly not let time and complacency ravage his body. She wasn't surprised. It was one of his weapons—considering the hard coil of muscle beneath her hand, probably one of his best.

Zane Edwards took everything seriously. For a moment, she had the urge to make him laugh. Really laugh. She wondered what it would be like, to hear him simply let go—of the pain, the guilt, the memories of death and destruction that he held on to. That all law-enforcement officers seemed to hold on to.

And if Elle was anything, it was impulsive. Giving in to the urge, she went straight for his ribs, digging her fingers in and tickling instead of teasing.

Zane jumped, but he didn't laugh. He didn't even chuckle.

His hand flattened her own against his skin, holding her prisoner. "What are you doing?"

"Tickling you."

"I'm not ticklish."

"Everyone is ticklish…somewhere."

"I'm not."

"Then let go of my hand."

"I don't think so. Besides, I have better plans for it."

"Nothing could be better than a good tickle fight."

His hand wrapped around hers, bringing it up his body. His head bent down, she could feel the pull of his shoulder and back muscles against her chest. She had to stand on tiptoe to keep her own shoulders from protesting the awkward movement. It only pulled her tighter against him.

His mouth touched her palm, a cascade of tingles exploding through her body. She undulated against him, an unconscious effort to get closer. A rumble of approval vibrated through him. She felt it everywhere—where his lips touched her, where his back caressed her breasts, where his rear pressed into the cradle of her thighs.

How could this man arouse her so completely and barely be touching her at all?

Her eyes were adjusting to the dark, able to pick out shades of gray. Shades of him.

Using his hold, he tugged her around to face him and began backing her through the room. His eyes smoldered with intensity. He was about to rock her world and she was about to let him.

She gulped, her throat suddenly dry. She wanted him to touch her, to please her, to fill her. And yet, that look in his eyes scared her.

It wasn't Zane necessarily, but the all-consuming way he gazed at her. As if everything in the world could be found inside her body. And that made what they were about to do much more important than she wanted it to be. If it was everything, then what would she do when it was over and he was gone?

What if she couldn't live up to his expectations? She hadn't felt this…insecurity in a very long time. This fear of disappointing someone who mattered.

For the past several years, she'd paraded through life, one experience after another. Wild. Exciting. The more outlandish and eccentric, the better. She wanted a store of life experiences to pull from—it made her a better artist. But none of the experiences—and none of the men she'd shared some of them with—had ever touched her. At least, not deeply. If something or someone didn't work, she moved on to the next adventure. Life was to be savored and experienced.

But Zane could touch her. Zane could matter. Zane could make her want things she shouldn't want to have, things that her experience had taught her would be bad.

Like a life with a driven, guilt-ridden, egotistical and demanding man.

Unfortunately, she was afraid that she already wanted those things, that man.

As the backs of her knees hit the mattress, she realized it was too late to do anything about it. He'd gotten under the defenses she'd built. He was already inside. And she was too far gone to push him back out again.

Her body tilted. Her core muscles engaged to fight gravity and keep her up. Zane's palm lifted to the center of her chest, his fingers spread between the valley of her breasts, the heat of him like an electrical surge in her blood.

One little push and she toppled over. Her body bounced against the mattress. She didn't move. He followed her down, wrapping his arm beneath her back and pulling her up higher as if her weight were insignificant.

She arched, her eyes slipping closed.

But he wouldn't let them stay that way. "Look at me." His voice was gravel, tight with control.

Her eyes popped open as he'd ordered, without her even realizing she would comply. His face was close to hers, his breath tickling the wisps of hair that had fallen from the upsweep she'd piled on the top of her head.

"I want you to look at me when I touch you. I want to see your eyes when I slide home. I want to watch them glaze over when you come. I want you to know who's fucking you. Not some guy from tonight. Not some guy from home."

With a growl in the back of his throat, Zane ripped her top down to her waist. She hadn't bothered with a bra, so when his lips latched on to her breast, there was nothing but heat and the moist suction of his mouth.

His hand kneaded the other side. His fingers pinched and pulled at one erect nipple while his teeth worried the other. She felt an answering tug deep inside her body, an ache that was quickly building to unbearable.

Her fingers buried in his hair, the silky strands of deep brown almost black in the darkness. They were soft against her skin, a contrast to the rough play of his hands over her body. His fingers were calloused. She wondered briefly what had caused them, certainly not playing with his guns. He was a man who wouldn't balk at hard work, if it needed to be done. He could get down and dirty if necessary.

She liked that about him. Hoped he was willing to get a little down and dirty with her.

Unwilling to sit passively by while he played her like a well-tuned fiddle, Elle yanked at his shirt, not caring if the seams ripped, as long as it revealed some skin.

The minute she'd torn his shirt off over his head, Zane went to work on her capris. He opened the zipper, but instead of pulling them off, he let his fingers play into the open V he'd revealed. He reached beneath the material, filling his hands with the curves of her ass, arching her body and pulling her aching sex closer to him. The bulge of his own arousal pressed against her hip, a tantalizing temptation. She squirmed in his hold, hoping to get him to shift and press it against her. She wanted to feel him, to rub against him and drive them both crazy. But he wouldn't let her.

His teeth nipped at her throat, sending the pulse point there racing.

But two could play. Lord, she wanted to play with him…. She reached for him, intent on yanking open his fly and filling her palm with the heat of him. But he pulled away from her, just out of reach.

She looked up into his face. Shadows shifted across his features, sharpening the blades of his cheekbones and making his lips appear fuller. She wanted to kiss them. And she wouldn't let him tease her this way. With a surge of her body, Elle rose beneath him. Her fingers wrapped around the waistband of his jeans and wouldn't let go.

She made quick work of his fly, but knew she'd never get the tight denim down his thighs unless he let her. Scrambling out from under him, Elle quickly shed her own pants and panties, shoving them into a pile on the floor that she'd deal with later. Much later.

She knelt on the bed; her thighs spread apart, her hands on her hips, a smirk touching her lips.

"Lose 'em, mister."

She'd never been shy with her body. When your grandmother was a nude model and you live in a house with three men, modesty just doesn't seem to have a place to survive. She'd sketched her first nude when she was barely seventeen. The woman had been overweight, with sagging breasts and the rounded belly of a mother who'd borne several children. She'd love to sketch Zane, the way his bones and muscles connected, the sinewy grace beneath that hard exterior. The fluidity that spoke to a man who knew his body and knew exactly what to do with it.

With quick precise motions, Zane shed his clothes, draping them over the arm of a chair instead of throwing them to the floor as she had. She probably should be grateful he hadn't stopped to fold them. At least, it gave her a moment to stare.

His erection jutted proudly from his body. A single bead of moisture glistened at the tip. Her tongue darted out to lick across her lips and his cock jerked in response. A fun little trick she'd have to remember for later.

With a surge of muscles and strength, Zane reached across the bed and pulled her back down beneath him. His hold on her was anything but soft. The intensity in his gaze sent a burst of uneasiness through her that was immediately replaced with a moan of desire when he clamped his mouth to hers again, his tongue plundering her in a way that only made her hungrier for the feel of him deep inside.

His arm hooked beneath her knee and pulled her thigh up into the air. Her body was open and exposed to him, hot, wet, ready.

The head of his penis scraped against the opening of her body. Her muscles quaked against the strain of holding back. She wanted him. She wanted it all. But he wouldn't give it to her.

Elle fumbled blindly in the nightstand beside the bed. She'd quietly asked the concierge for condoms this afternoon, feeling more like a naughty teenager now than she had even when she was a naughty teenager. She grabbed a handful, letting the others rain back down until she held a single one between her fingers.

With her teeth, she tore savagely into it, letting the broken foil flutter to the floor. Her other hand found his hot flesh wedged between them. He was so close to her sex that the back of her hand brushed against her own wet heat drawing a hiss of pleasure from between her lips.

Her fingers stroked up and down his length. She spread the moisture she found there over the head of him, enjoying the way his body jerked as she played across the sensitive tip.

"I told you I'd find the right spot," she whispered, her voice husky with satisfaction.

"This isn't a game," he growled. His eyes, suddenly smoky and dark, held her captive. For a moment, she worried he could see straight to her soul, straight to the vulnerable place he was building inside her. She needed this to be a game.

But she knew that it wasn't and, no matter how hard she tried to make it that, it never would be.

Elle tore her eyes from him, concentrating on the condom she rolled slowly over his cock. He was hard and hot and her body throbbed with the need to have him fill her. But she still found herself whispering the question she never should have let out into the universe. "Then what is it?"

Because she was so afraid of his answer.

He plunged deep inside, invading her body and forcing a cry of pleasure from her that she'd had no intention of giving up. With smooth, long strokes, he claimed her, and she couldn't find the strength to care about the answer. She wanted him to take her. She wanted to be his.

He tortured them both. Pulling out slowly before sliding back in. Over and over again, Zane brought her to the brink of ecstasy, only to steal it away before she could grasp it with both hands.

Her body writhed beneath him, matching him stroke for stroke and silently begging him to put them both out of their misery. And still, he pushed her on for more. Her hands grappled against his sweat-slicked skin, trying to find a purchase that would force him closer and hold him to her forever.

Her muscles quivered with strain and anticipation. Pleasure flooded her system, her mind spinning out into empty space, unable to grasp anything but the relentless need he was building inside. A final claiming stroke vaulted her into the strongest orgasm of her life. She'd heard women talk about seeing stars. She'd thought they'd lied. She'd been wrong.

Light burst behind her eyelids. Her fingernails dug into his flesh and raked shakily down his back, trying to find something to hold on to in the middle of the storm.

With the half a brain cell that still functioned, Elle registered Zane's own grunt of release, the way his body shuddered above her as he finally let go. The friction was sensational against her contracting muscles, pulling that last fraction of pleasure out of the moment.

Damn, he was good. But then she'd known he would be. Zane Edwards was the type of man who wouldn't settle for mediocre. He excelled at everything he did—including sex.

He collapsed beside her, careful not to crush her beneath the weight of his body. She wouldn't have cared if he had. Breathing was overrated anyway.

She sank down into the comfort and calm after the storm. She listened as his labored breaths slowed to something resembling normal. Satisfaction and bone-clenching fear rolled around inside her, confusing her brain and her body. How could she feel so content and so scared all at the same time?

Elle tried to banish the thoughts, not wanting to ruin whatever time she had with Zane on regrets and worry over something she couldn't change. She had plenty of time to analyze and pick apart her decisions tomorrow. Tonight, she wanted to sink into his body and enjoy the warmth of the moment between them.

Zane was so still, the even expansion and contraction of his body lulling her into thinking that he'd fallen asleep. Until his quiet voice whispered against her ear. "I don't know what this is. All I know is that I wanted to be there tonight, which is why I stayed away."

His words both scared her further and sent a warm fuzzy feeling coursing through her veins. Or maybe that was just post-sex satisfaction.

The problem was, if he didn't know what this was, how was she supposed to know? Oh, she had no doubt this was trouble, the schoolgirl flutter of her heart was enough to tell her that.

But she was so afraid that it was more. No one—no man—had ever made her feel this way. This vulnerable and excited and horny and scared. An addictive mixture that had apparently gone straight to her head.

The real question was, what would she do when it and he were gone?

10

AFTER ANOTHER AMAZING round, Zane had fallen asleep. Elle was exhausted, but she couldn't seem to settle.

No, it was more than that. Her guilty conscience wouldn't let her relax. Her imagination seemed to take the plain white key card still in the pocket of her crumpled capris and make it flashing neon. She'd been too scared to leave the thing in her room—even buried in a drawer—worried he'd come in and find it.

Why hadn't he mentioned it by now?

This was the perfect opportunity, in the middle of the quiet night, to rid herself of the risk and the guilt. Picking up his arm, she unwrapped it from around her waist and placed it gently onto the bed. He made a deep sound in the back of his throat but didn't wake.

Elle waited for several seconds, her nerves jangling the entire time, until he resettled. Then she quietly rose from the bed and, with stealthy fingers, reached into the pocket of her capris. The creak of floorboards beneath her feet as she crouched made her grimace, but she quickly found Zane's jeans and slipped the card into his back pocket.

There, it was done. Standing up, she stared across at the man lying in her bed, the guilt not quite gone. Relief now mixed with it, though, so she'd take what she could get. The familiar jitter of spent adrenaline pumped through her body, making sleep impossible. Her fingers itched to hold a charcoal or brush so that her mind could zone out.

Instead of turning on a light, Elle opened the curtains that Zane had closed when he'd snuck into her room.

She realized that she should probably be upset with him for that bold move, but considering aftershocks of pleasure kept randomly shooting through her body, she really wasn't angry he'd been waiting for her.

Elle grabbed her sketch pad and her box of charcoals before settling into the chair closest to the window. Moonlight poured into the room, washing across his body and gilding him with silvery shadows.

He was peaceful. The most peaceful she'd ever seen him. The harsh lines that dug into the middle of his forehead and bracketed his mouth had almost disappeared. Those lines weren't from age—they were all stress. Stress and the burden of seeing too much, more than any one person should ever have to deal with. Her brothers, probably only a few years younger than Zane, carried the same badges of their job.

Again, she wondered what he was doing here, buried in the middle of nowhere. What was his story? What had happened? Because she'd been around the law-enforcement life long enough to realize that something had. Inexplicably, she wanted him to share that with her, whatever had put those lines on his face. She wanted to be his sounding board, to understand and share the burden.

Something she'd sworn she'd never do in a million years.

Her life had been the opposite of what it was supposed to be. Most cop families lived in fear that they'd get that call one day that their loved one had been killed in the line of duty. She hadn't gotten that call. Instead, at five, she'd learned her mother was dying a slow and painful death. She'd watched her struggle with the ravages of cancer on her body.

She'd lost one parent and still had to live with the daily fear that she'd lose the other one.

She'd attended funerals for her father's comrades, seen the tears and grief. And she'd promised herself she wouldn't live each day in fear for another man in her life. After her father and brothers, she didn't have any room on the list for someone else.

She wanted a man who wasn't a hero. Who wouldn't put the safety of others above the safety of himself.

And that was all a lie. Of course she wanted a hero. A man with the same honor and integrity her father had. A man who lived up to the lofty example her father had set for her.

A man like Zane.

Her father would definitely approve of Zane. He wouldn't approve of what she'd done over the past few days. Breaking and entering, pickpocketing…

Closing her eyes tight for several seconds, Elle tried to will away the ache that had started somewhere close to her heart.

There were so many reasons why this was a bad idea. But the fact that he was asleep in her bed meant that those reasons didn't carry much weight. At least, not with her heart.

She sighed. *Damn it.* How could she have fallen for him so quickly?

Her eyes opened again. They traveled across his body, viewing him not just as an artist but as someone who cared.

She supposed the real question was, what woman wouldn't fall for Zane? He was selfless, determined, beautiful.

His body was almost diagonal across the bed, his torso encroaching on the spot she'd vacated. The white hotel sheet was draped low across his hips, and one of his feet was sticking out the other side. She wasn't sure if it was deliberate or if the position he was in made the cotton sheet too short to cover his body.

Her fingers moved languidly across the page, soft gray lines and sharp shadowed angles appearing beneath her sure strokes. Her fingers brushed across his back, smudging the reproduction of the scars she could see there. Puckered flesh long healed, still held memories of experiences he hadn't shared with her.

When she was finished, she stared down at the contrast of him. Soft, dreamy moonlight, relaxed muscles, peaceful sleep and those ripping scars across his flesh.

A lump in her throat, Elle stood up from the chair and placed the pad in the seat. Exhaustion and the overwhelming urge to be next to him, skin to skin, stole over her. Her arms felt so heavy and her eyes were suddenly gritty and bone-dry.

With a sigh, Elle climbed into bed, gently picked Zane's arm up and snugged it back around her. He made another sound, pulling her closer against his body.

Without really awakening, he mumbled, "Everything okay?" his words slurring with sleep.

"Fine," she said, her own speech heavy and tired.

Three seconds later, she was out.

When she woke, she was alone. Not surprising, considering the clock on her bedside table said it was well past ten. She hadn't slept that late in a very long time. She might be an artist at the whim of her creative impulses, but after years with her father living on a strict schedule...old habits died hard. She supposed that vacation was as good a time as any to sleep in. Especially given how late into the morning she'd been up.

She lay in bed for a little while, wondering what Zane was doing and whether or not she'd see him today. Once again, he'd left without giving her anything. She tried to reason with herself. This wasn't back home. This wasn't the start of a relationship. He didn't owe her anything—least of all, the reassurance that they'd share a repeat performance of the previous evening.

Her eyes darted around the room anyway, looking for a note he might have left her. There wasn't one. Elle tried not to let the disappointment ruin the residual glow from last night.

She wondered briefly what she should do today. There were ballroom lessons; she'd always wanted to learn the tango. But, really, the thought of some other man having his arms wrapped around her made her cringe. Now, if she could convince Zane to go with her... She could just imagine his stiff body going languid with the sexual thrill of the dance. Desire began to simmer. Instead of letting it take hold, she pushed it away. Another thought for another time.

She could always paint, but today the thought of lugging everything out to the beach simply had no appeal.

She finally settled on eating a late breakfast, changing into her swimsuit, grabbing the floppy-brimmed hat she'd packed at the last minute and spending the day lying in the sand. It had been a very long time since she'd read a book.

As she was digging into her suitcase, the sound of crumpling paper stopped her cold. Flipping a few things out of her way, Elle uncovered the picture that had started her headlong flight to Escape.

Nana's picture stared back at her accusingly. Deep despair, the same emotion she'd felt on the day she'd lost the painting, welled up inside. Her grandmother seemed to look out of the portrait and straight into her soul.

Elle realized she was the one adding accusation to the mischievous eyes, but that didn't stop the feeling from cutting deep. She had failed, but she had no idea how to correct that problem.

Her conscience wouldn't let her do anything illegal, at least not again. In fact, she could hear Nana's voice in the back of her head now… "Two wrongs do not make a right, young lady."

Perhaps she should just talk to Marcy. Tell her the truth of why she'd come to the island. Before, Elle had been reluctant to pay to retrieve the painting. It was hers by rights. She shouldn't have to pay for the return of something that was already hers.

But she had the money. When she got to the island, the painting had been the most important thing. Now, her integrity and Zane's opinion of her were equally so.

She'd also assumed that her unanswered emails and letters had been because the owner had full knowledge of the fact that it was stolen art. However, now that she was here, she didn't think that was true.

If nothing else, Simon struck her as an intelligent man who wouldn't flaunt his stolen property in the pages of a travel magazine with worldwide distribution.

And if he wasn't smart enough to realize the danger in that, Marcy was.

Elle needed to think about it, though. Starting today, she was going to turn over a new leaf. Think about things before she rushed into them.

Better late than never.

IT HAD BEEN ONE HELL OF A day. The alarm on Zane's phone had woken him at 6:00 a.m. Bleary-eyed, he'd stumbled from Elle's room back to his own place so he could change clothes and relieve Tom. He'd wanted nothing more than to stay right where he was, his body wrapped around the warmth of her, but he couldn't.

Wouldn't let himself give in to the weakness of needing to stay.

He'd started the day grouchy and it had gone downhill from there. A guest had claimed that a piece of jewelry had gone missing from her room. It was the first time they'd ever had a report of theft on the property since he'd been there, and if Elle hadn't been wrapped in his arms all night, he might have been tempted to accuse her of the crime. The situation had certainly fit her M.O. He knew she was innocent, and had promised as much to Marcy when she'd asked if Elle could be involved. He'd ignored the tiny spurt of relief when he'd reviewed the tapes and discovered no one but the guest herself had exited or entered her room.

After several of the staff searched the room, one of the maids found the diamond bracelet wedged between the dresser and the wall.

Crisis averted—after about five hours of drama and one hell of a headache. He'd been so preoccupied that he didn't even have a clue where Elle was or how she'd spent her day.

He practically stumbled back to his bungalow, cringing at the sight of his clothes from last night strewn across the bed, where he'd left them this morning.

Picking them up, he'd intended to throw them in the hamper where they belonged, but stopped short when something hard stabbed into his hand. A frown marring his face, he dug into the back pocket and pulled out his missing key card. It had definitely not been there last night. His mind raced as he tried to determine when she might have slipped it back into his pocket, but he realized with disgust that she could have done it whenever she wanted. He'd been so preoccupied with getting his hands on her again, a bomb could have exploded in the next room and he would have ignored it.

Yanking his cell from his belt, he hit the button to call the Crow's Nest.

He didn't even wait for Tom to acknowledge him, instead rumbling, "Where is she?"

"Uh…who?" the other man stuttered over the crackling connection.

"Ms. Monroe. Where is she? And what has she been doing today?"

"How should I—"

"Find out."

The other man sputtered, "But I wasn't on—"

"Use the face-recognition software to find out where she is right now and then track her movements for today and get back to me."

"Yes, sir."

The software was a little gift Simon had given him several months ago. Unlike casinos, which were constantly looking for banned players and known card counters, Escape seldom used it. However, Zane had wanted it available in case they ever needed to track the resort for suspected criminals or terrorists. He'd used it a few times over the past week to track Elle's movements, not that he'd shared that with anyone, including Tom.

The cell in his hand crackled as Tom opened the line. "Sir, she's in her room. Well, that's the last time the system picked her up, about an hour ago."

Excellent. "Track her movements and get back to me. I want to know everything, including what she had for breakfast, lunch and dinner."

"Sir, I don't think she's eaten dinner yet."

"I don't care," he barked into the phone, punching the button that ended their call.

Slipping the accusing card into the pocket of his jeans, Zane forgot all about being exhausted, the shower he'd wanted and his plans for the night.

He wasn't sure what he felt. Anger was definitely in the mix, but it was aimed more at himself than anything. How had he let himself get so distracted by lust that he hadn't noticed her put the card back?

And he was confused. Why had she taken the card, only to return it unused? He knew for certain that she hadn't used it. He'd checked the system before heading to her room last night, and if it was sitting in his pocket now, that meant it had been there when he'd left this morning. She hadn't had the opportunity.

He wanted to shake her, and yell at her and ask her what the hell she was doing—and hope that this time she actually answered him. He was frustrated, that's what he was. He wanted her to be honest with him, so that he could stop her from doing something stupid. Something else stupid.

He knew she had a secret, and he was tired of waiting for her to let him in. He was tired of her lies and her games. He wanted answers. And he was going to get them.

A LOUD, INSISTENT KNOCK sounded on Elle's door. She paused, staring at the panel for several seconds.

"I know you're in there, Elle. Let me in."

The tight tone in Zane's voice had Elle's stomach turning, the confrontation she'd expected all day finally here. A buzz of expectation had haunted her every step today. Part of her was relieved that it was finally here and they could just deal with it and get on with…whatever was left when this was over.

Crossing the room, she opened the door.

Zane stood framed in the doorway, a mix of emotions clouding his eyes. They strayed long enough to rake down her body, taking in her damp hair and the silk robe she'd thrown on after her shower. But instead of suffusing with passion as she might have hoped, the depth in his eyes sharpened and swirled. Not good.

Pushing past her, Zane spun in the center of the room to watch as she quietly closed the door. His body was tight, not in an explosive way but with…an angry tension that didn't give her a lot of hope.

"What are you doing, Elle? Why are you here?"

The chasm between them suddenly seemed bigger than the length of the room that actually separated them. She looked at him, unblinking, wanting to tell him the truth. But she'd been keeping her reason for being here a secret for so long she wasn't sure how. How could she tell him without creating irreparable damage?

Impatient, Zane dug into his pocket and pulled out

the white card. He held it in front of his face, letting it dangle from the plastic tab and anchor clip for several seconds.

"Would you like to explain this?"

Swallowing, she forced herself to answer calmly. "Well, it looks like your all-access key card."

"And how did it end up back in my pocket?"

"I put it there."

That seemed to surprise him, cutting off a protesting growl in midrumble, almost as if he'd expected her to lie and had come preloaded with the proper response. His mouth snapped shut and he stared at her for several seconds, no doubt regrouping, and then asked, "You're not denying that you took it?"

She crossed her arms over her chest in a protective gesture, a move that showed the weakness she didn't want him to see.

"No, why would I? We both know I took it. And you also know I didn't use it. I could have, but I didn't."

His eyes filled with confusion, frustration, hope and a tinge of anger. "Why, Elle? Why did you take it? Make me understand."

She wanted to do that, so much it hurt. She wanted to make the accusation in his eyes disappear. But there were no magical words, because he had every right to be upset with her.

Before he could react, the phone at his hip beeped and another voice filled the room. "Sir, she grabbed a banana and apple from the breakfast buffet, spent all day on the beach with a book and then went upstairs. No lunch, no dinner."

Snatching the phone from his hip, he said, "Thanks," before punching the end call button and replacing it. His eyes didn't waver from hers at all.

"If you wanted to know what I did today, why didn't you just ask me?"

"Because I wasn't sure I'd get the truth."

"Touché," she said, a tinge of sadness coloring the word. She couldn't argue with him, because she'd given him every reason to doubt her.

Plopping onto the bed, Elle was suddenly very tired. Tired of fighting with him, tired of the dance.

As if sensing her weariness and weakness, Zane pressed, "Why did you take it?"

"So I could access the private areas." She looked up at him from across the room. "I would have thought that was obvious."

"Why didn't you?"

"Because I felt like shit for taking it."

Some of the tension seemed to leak out of his body. He stared at her for several more seconds before taking another step toward her.

"What were you hoping to find?"

She knew it had been coming to this. She knew the minute she put that card back into his pocket that she'd have to tell him the truth. Was actually looking forward to telling him the truth. It would be a relief to not have secrets anymore.

Standing up from the bed, she walked around to his side of the room. She tried to ignore the way he shifted his weight out of her reach so that they wouldn't touch as she scooted past him toward the dresser.

She picked up the piece of paper she'd left lying there. Holding it out to him, she said, "This."

He grasped the page and studied it. Furrows of confusion etched deeper grooves across the bridge of his nose. "The magazine ad? What does that have to do with anything?"

"It's the reason I'm here."

Zane looked up at her, the glossy page crumpling beneath his fingers. "Marcy will be glad to hear the marketing campaign is working."

"That's not what I meant." Elle fought the urge to move closer to him, knowing he wouldn't want her in his personal space right now. Instead, she curled her fingers over the edge of the dresser behind her, using it as an anchor. The sharp edge pressed into her back, the biting pain a sort of penance for the sins she'd committed in the name of her grandmother's painting.

"The painting."

Zane returned his gaze to the page, the furrows getting deeper. "What about it?"

"The woman is my grandmother. The painting is mine. It was stolen from me four years ago."

11

"What do you mean, the painting is yours?"

Zane watched as Elle sank onto the bed. Her seemingly inexhaustible supply of energy having deserted her, leaving her listless. Heartbroken.

"The artist was my grandmother's lover before she met my grandfather. He gave the painting to her before they parted ways."

Her fingers played in her lap, wrapping and unwrapping around each other as she stared sightlessly into the tangled mess.

"I don't expect you to understand." But she looked up at him beseechingly, her eyes filled with equal parts hopelessness and a blazing faith he wasn't sure she should place in him.

"I'm not sure anyone can understand how important Nana was to me. My mom died when I was five. My father and two older brothers raised me. They're all cops. They were controlling and exacting and unforgiving. They were hard to live with, especially for a precocious, creative child who just wanted the freedom to explore and experience life."

Zane could hear the mingled frustration and affection in her voice as she spoke of the men who comprised her family.

"Nana was the only one who understood me. She... could identify with the little girl who wanted to dip her fingers in paint and rub them across her bedroom walls." She laughed, a tiny explosion, at the memory. "My father just bellowed. I don't even remember him actually saying any words."

Her eyes raised to his again. "Don't get me wrong. I love them. It was just difficult for us all to live together.

"Nana was my rock, the one person I could cry to. The one person who understood me when I couldn't see through my anger and frustration to remember that I loved the big oafs who protected me even if I didn't want them to.

"She died when I was sixteen. That painting—" she gestured to the paper still clutched in his hand "—is the only thing of hers that I had left. It was stolen several years ago, along with anything else valuable that I owned. The rest of the stuff was replaceable. Not that painting. I thought I'd lost it forever."

Her eyes lifted to him once more, only this time they glistened with the sheen of unshed tears. She gritted her teeth, refusing to let the tears fall. She might not realize it, but she had more of her father and brothers in her than she probably wanted to admit. Their tenacity. Strength. Determination. Stubbornness.

Oh, yeah, he'd seen plenty of that over the past few days. Unfortunately, pairing those things with her impulsive nature could spell disaster.

He'd lived through disaster once. Shaking his head, Zane realized he wasn't sure he could live through it again. The last time, that tragedy had been all his fault.

He could have prevented it, should have prevented it. That knowledge gave him a small measure of comfort. If he'd played by the rules, then Felicity would be alive.

Elle, he couldn't control. Hell, no one could.

The methodical agent with an inherent need to gather the details surfaced, a guy he'd been suppressing for months. Questions, angles and possibilities began to swim around inside his head. "So why don't you file paperwork and ask for it back?"

Her lips began to tremble. She pressed them together to hide the weakness.

"I can't prove that it's mine. My lawyer said without documentation, a bill of sale or a will or something, then I don't have a leg to stand on. The painting was a gift to Nana. The artist wasn't anywhere close to famous at the time. She never thought to get anything saying it had been given to her. Nana didn't have a will. The only thing of value that she owned was that painting and it was already hanging on the wall in my father's home since she lived with us after my mother died. My father simply handed it to me so that I could hang it in my room and remember her. The only thing I have is a police report the night it was stolen listing it as various wall art."

Zane looked at her. He wanted to help. What warm-blooded man wouldn't? He could see how important the painting was to her. But he couldn't make any promises…not yet. He couldn't get her hopes up, only to see them dashed again. He needed more information.

"Why didn't you contact Simon?"

"I tried!" she exclaimed, hopping up from the bed. For the first time since she began her story, he saw her frustration. He also saw the sparkle of life that he'd come to associate with Elle, that glistening intent in her eyes that said she was up to something, something reckless and probably dangerous.

"He ignored my emails. My letters went unanswered. Even my phone messages weren't returned."

Yep, that sounded like Simon, who'd probably had his nose buried in the keyboard and didn't even realize he'd ignored Elle's attempts at communication.

"I assumed he was fully aware that the painting was stolen and was ignoring me on purpose."

More likely, his best friend hadn't looked very closely at the paperwork—or lack thereof—that had come with said painting. Simon was brilliant at what he did, but he had a tendency toward tunnel vision.

Zane cringed at the thought of the paperwork he might or might not have attached to the painting.

"Elle, I'm sorry, but I can't promise you anything." And he wanted to. He wanted to gather her in his arms and tell her everything was going to be okay. But at this moment, he couldn't do that. He needed to talk to Simon, figure out how the painting had gotten on his wall and the details that went along with the sale.

Elle looked back down at her hands. The fingers were twisted together again, but they'd gone still in her lap. She gulped—he could see her throat undulate as she fought to control her emotions. But despite her efforts, a single tear plopped down onto her entwined fingers.

In a thick voice, she said, "I didn't think you would."

SHE'D WATCHED IN SILENCE as he walked out her door. The night had not ended the way she'd hoped. Instead of sharing the bed with Zane, she was sitting alone in the dark, the center of her chest aching from an unproductive bout of tears and a pain she was deeply afraid meant she'd let him break her heart.

It shouldn't hurt as much as it did. She hadn't expected him to believe her. She'd given Zane Edwards every reason *not* to believe her. She'd broken into guest rooms. She'd stolen his key card. She'd lied to him repeatedly.

And she'd fallen in love with the man.

She realized that the deck—and laws—were stacked against her. Ultimately, that was the reason she'd come here with the intent to "reacquire" the painting in the first place. She knew there was no other choice. She couldn't prove the painting belonged to her, so she couldn't blame Zane—or Simon—for not volunteering to hand it over.

They had no reason to believe her.

That painting belonged to her, damn it. She wanted it back, although a certain amount of heat had disappeared from her conviction. It hurt to think that she might leave the island empty-handed—no painting, no Zane. But she feared that was exactly what was going to happen.

She'd never really had Zane to begin with. How could she have? They'd just met. Yet her heart had plummeted straight into choppy seas without her even realizing it.

At the end of all this, she would go home and he would stay here, buried in a tropical paradise that was choking him to death.

She might not be able to take the painting home with her, but she would like to see it one more time. Was that so much to ask? Elle didn't think so.

But she was done taking the difficult approach.

She didn't want to ask Zane. She didn't want to put

him in a position where he felt he'd have to tell her
no. That would be painful for them both. Instead, she
thought of Marcy, the woman who'd been friendly, ac-
commodating and infinitely knowledgeable about what
went on around her.

Elle picked the magazine ad up off the dresser where
Zane had left it. Hadn't Zane told her Marcy was the
one behind the ad to begin with? There was no doubt
she'd know where the painting hung.

Elle turned to leave, but stopped when her sad and
sunken eyes caught her own reflection in the mirror.
She looked like a bedraggled rat. Not a very flattering
visual in the least.

She took a few minutes to cover up the evidence
of her crying jag. She couldn't completely hide the
bloodshot eyes and red-tinged nose, but some con-
cealer, powder and blush made it look as if she'd spent
a little too much time in the sun and at the bar instead
of sprawled across her bed, losing her mind.

Full of resolve, she marched down to the front desk
and asked for Marcy.

The director came out of the back with a fake smile
on her face that turned genuine when she saw Elle waiting for her. Marcy crossed to the far end of the desk,
pulling them both out of earshot of the woman working there. The same one who'd been on duty when she
and Zane had trooped in soaking wet.

"Elle, what can I do for you?"

Elle placed the paper onto the counter between them,
smoothed out the wrinkled edges and asked, "Do you
know where this painting is?"

"Certainly."

Elle waited for more, but none came. It wasn't lost

on her that Marcy had answered her question with no intention of actually telling her anything.

"Is there any way I could see it?"

A frown marred Marcy's forehead and tipped her lips downward. "I'm sorry, but it's in one of the private offices."

It was no more than she'd expected to learn. She'd pretty much narrowed down the painting's resting place to somewhere she couldn't normally gain access to.

"Marcy, I'm going to be honest with you. I came here to see this painting. It has sentimental value to me."

"What do you mean?"

Elle's gaze shifted down to Nana's face. "She's my grandmother."

Marcy's eyes widened for a moment, glancing between the picture and Elle. "You have the same eyes."

Elle nodded, silently fighting against the tight lump in her throat.

"Is that why you broke into those rooms?"

Elle straightened her shoulders and met Marcy's gaze directly. "Yes."

"Well, that was a waste of time. This sort of artwork wouldn't be in one of the guest rooms."

"I figured that out."

"Why didn't you just ask?"

She sighed. "That's a long story. Suffice it to say, I didn't think anyone would admit to me that it was here."

"Sort of difficult to deny it when the evidence is plastered in full-page color."

It was Elle's turn to frown. Marcy had a point, but she really didn't feel like admitting she'd originally intended to steal the painting.

"Let's just say I had my reasons."

Elle looked down at the paper sitting on the polished

wooden counter between them. She reached a single fingertip and rubbed it over the reproduction of her grandmother's face. Tears she thought had been completely spent began to gather and sting at the back of her throat. She pushed them back.

"I know I don't deserve it, but I would really appreciate it if I could see the painting. That's all I'm asking for."

Marcy stared at her for several seconds. She probed Elle's gaze, but Elle refused to flinch.

"I'll see what I can do. I might be able to get you a few minutes later tonight."

"Thank you," Elle breathed, reaching across and grasping the other woman's hand.

"Don't hold your breath. Simon's supposed to go to the mainland tonight, which means his office would be free. But he often changes plans at the last second. And if he stays, there's no way in hell I'm going to let you into his office. Not even if you were the queen."

"I understand."

Elle walked away, feeling giddy. Not euphoric, more like she'd just gone cliff diving and couldn't believe she'd lived to tell the tale. She was finally going to see the painting again, after all these years. See her Nana.

She would have thought the only thing she'd be was excited.

What she hadn't expected was the layer of disappointment and sadness that accompanied the realization that whatever happened, her time here was almost over.

ZANE BARGED INTO SIMON'S office without knocking. It was a big no-no, even for him. He didn't care. He needed some answers and he needed them now.

Simon looked up from the monitors that sat on his desk, shielding him from the world. When he was working his focus narrowed to the two screens.

How Marcy thought Simon played online games and poker all day, Zane would never understand. Maybe it was because that's what Simon wanted her to think.

"What the hell are you doing?" Simon growled. His eyes were bleary. The man probably hadn't slept in forever. Now that he thought about it, Zane hadn't seen Simon for the past twenty-four hours.

"I need to ask you a couple of questions."

"Can't this wait? I'm a little busy right now." Simon gestured toward the computer.

"No. No, it can't."

Zane's gaze traveled around the room, zeroing in on the painting on the far side that hung between matching bookshelves.

It had always been there, but Zane had never really looked at it. Hadn't had a reason to. And when he walked into this room, it was usually with an agenda.

The photo in the magazine didn't do it justice.

He walked closer, ignoring the sputtered sound of exasperation behind him. The painting was striking. Not just because of the rich color palette the artist had used—gold, crimson, browns so deep they were almost black. There was a connection, ostensibly between the artist and the model staring out of the canvas over her shoulder. But the direct gaze of the woman brought everyone into that moment. Her welcoming eyes, full of mischief and desire and promise…

Zane felt a tug deep in the center of his body as he stared at the woman with the deep red robe wrapped partway around her, trailing off her shoulders as if she would drop it at any moment.

Desire shot through him. For a second he was seriously weirded out. He'd never had that reaction to a painting in his life. He'd seen nudes before. Taken art history as an elective in college. Not to mention the fact that the woman currently turning him on was the grandmother of his lover.

And then he realized something. It was the eyes. They were Elle's.

The bright gray eyes. They were unusual. Arresting. In person and on canvas.

And it was proof to him that Elle had been telling the truth—although he hadn't really needed any. From the moment she'd raised her tear-glazed eyes as she'd told her story, he'd known she was being truthful. Finally.

"Where did you get this painting?"

"I don't know." The impatience oozing out of Simon didn't help Zane's temper.

"Damn it, Simon. Am I Marcy?"

"Noo." His friend drew out the single syllable, probably wondering where the trick was and how the question was relevant.

If there was anything that Simon loved, it was solving puzzles. It was one reason he was such a good thriller writer.

"Do I interrupt you on a regular basis?"

"Well…"

"Let me rephrase. Do I interrupt you with needless concerns or unimportant details?"

"You mean, aside from the redhead you handcuffed to a chair, oh, and disappearing into the jungle with her and scaring the hell out of half the staff?"

It was Zane's turn to growl.

"Fine. No, you are one of the few people who do not

interrupt me for the sheer pleasure of watching steam pour out of my ears."

Triumph in his voice, Zane said, "So, can we just skip the preliminaries and agree that I wouldn't be here if this wasn't important?"

Simon narrowed his eyes for several seconds, turned his attention back to the computer only long enough to close out whatever he'd been working on and then leaned back in his chair. Zane now had his full attention.

"Where did you get this painting?"

"My decorator showed it to me."

"Where did your decorator find it?"

"I don't know. I didn't play twenty questions. She showed it to me. I liked it. I bought it. She had it hung in my office. I decided it wasn't appropriate for downstairs in the guest areas."

"Why not? I mean, aren't we really selling sex?"

"No, Mr. Cynical. We are selling a fantasy. Sex is sometimes a result. But not always. You certainly haven't indulged in the favorite island pastime…until recently."

His friend leaned even farther back in his chair, clasping his hands behind his head and lounging in a deceptively relaxed pose.

"Screw you. And stop changing the subject."

"I wasn't the one who changed it, my friend. You're the one who brought up sex. I'm wondering if that's because you aren't getting enough, or can't stop thinking about getting more."

Zane decided to ignore him and the truth behind his words. "The painting. Were there any papers? Did the decorator provide provenance?"

"Provide what?"

"Provenance. Proof of ownership. Proof that the painting was legitimate. Clean. Not stolen."

"Not that I remember. But then, I was a little preoccupied at the time. She might have and I just didn't pay attention."

Which didn't shock Zane in the least.

"What is this all about, Zane?"

"Someone has made a claim that this painting is stolen."

"How do they even know that I have it?"

Zane looked at him incredulously, fighting the urge to smack Simon upside the head. "Did you even look at the ad Marcy spent so much time and energy on?"

"No. Why would I? That's her job. And she's more than capable of handling it. Why would I hire someone and then micromanage every little thing they do? That's just silly."

"So is buying a painting without knowing if it could be legally sold or not."

"I can't imagine my decorator would buy stolen property." The small smile that curled the edges of Simon's lips made Zane want to cringe.

"You slept with her, didn't you?"

"Who?"

"The decorator!"

"Yeah. She was beautiful and a hell of a lay."

"Jesus, Simon. When are you going to grow up? College was a long time ago."

"I don't know, Zane. When are you going to have the stick up your ass surgically removed?"

Zane's back teeth rubbed together. A headache the size of Texas accompanied the molar friction.

"I need to see any paperwork that you have, Simon. Preferably now."

"Fine." Standing, Simon walked across to the shelves. The bottom half of both contained drawers that held files. As Simon pulled the far left one open, Zane saw the neat tabs with their perfect handwriting and knew Marcy had organized everything inside. Which was a good thing. It meant that Simon might actually be able to find what he needed. Before next week.

While he was waiting, Zane's gaze skimmed across Simon's line of books. Every subject imaginable was represented. Antiques, archaeology, psychology, weapons, terrorism, law, evidence. And art. Almost an entire shelf dedicated to art, art theft, famous heists, unsolved cases.

Zane's gaze swung back to his friend. For a brief moment, he wondered how well he really knew the man. They'd lived in each other's back pockets during college, but that was years ago.

Zane shook his head. There was a rational explanation as to why Simon had those books on his shelf. And he knew what it was. The same reason weapons books lined the shelf below—research.

"There." Simon held out a crisp manila folder labeled Art Acquisitions 2009. "Whatever you need should be in there. If it isn't, I don't have it."

Zane spun on his heel, grasping the folder tightly in his fist. He was almost to the door when Simon's voice stopped him. "Zane, I'm assuming you'll take care of this for me? I really don't have time for interruptions right now." The languid, careless tone that always permeated his friend's voice had disappeared, leaving behind an edge of desperation that Zane didn't often hear from Simon.

"Yeah. I'll take care of it."

"Thanks. I'll be on the mainland tonight, but I'll be

back in the morning if you need anything else. And I promise not to snarl at you…much…if you interrupt. I really hate to think that I bought a stolen painting. If it belongs to someone else, I want to know."

And there was the core of the man Zane knew. Underneath the disinterested exterior, beat the heart of a man with integrity, drive and passion.

Damn it. How had they all gotten into this mess?

Zane took the folder to the Crow's Nest. After waving Tom back into the seat before the monitors, he opened it up and began flipping through the pages. They'd acquired many pieces of art in 2009. He recognized several of the paintings he'd shown Elle a few days ago.

What he was looking for was buried close to the back. A single piece of paper was stapled to a picture of the painting. That was it. A bill of sale, with nothing more.

Completely unhelpful. He honestly wasn't sure what he'd hoped to find. He believed Elle's story, but he had enough experience with the legal system to know that her lawyer was right—no court would award her the painting, since she couldn't prove it was hers. Simon's paperwork might be flimsy, but it would hold up against nothing.

He could always ask his friend to give Elle the painting. Hell, Simon would probably do it without blinking an eye. But Zane wasn't sure how he felt about that. Was it wrong? Was it right? Could he ask his friend to give up a painting worth thousands of dollars just so that he could see the smile on Elle's face?

For the first time in a long time, Zane faced a decision that wasn't black-and-white. Dread tightened his stomach for a moment. The last time he'd had to make a tough decision, he'd made the wrong one, and Felicity had paid the price.

But this wasn't life and death. It was just a painting, one that meant so much to Elle but probably nothing at all to Simon. He'd talk to his friend—ask him to consider selling the painting to Elle. Or giving it to her. Or whatever Simon felt was right. He'd do it tomorrow when Simon returned—he'd probably already left, or was getting ready to leave, and wouldn't be very receptive.

In the meantime, Zane had the overwhelming urge to see Elle, to hold her and touch her. The vision of her sitting on her bed, a tear rolling down her face, made his chest tighten all over again. He wouldn't mention his plan to her, not until he'd talked to Simon. He had no idea what his boss would do and the last thing he wanted was to get Elle's hopes up, only to see them dashed again.

12

ELLE HAD TIME TO KILL, SO she decided to jump in the shower and stay there until her fingers were pruny. She washed her hair, conditioned it twice and took her time spreading the coconut-and-floral body wash the resort had supplied over her skin.

She closed her eyes, tipped her head back and let the hot water stream over her face and body.

You'd think in a tropical location she'd have preferred a dip in the pool, but she really didn't. The heat and cloud of moisture seemed to insulate her as nothing else could.

Which was probably why she didn't realize Zane was there until his hand reached through the fog and pulled open the glass door. Steam swirled out as a chill leaked in.

Elle jerked around in the spray, sending rivulets of water cascading onto the stone floor. Her breath backed up into her lungs. A yearning so deep it made her ache took up residence inside her chest. It made her angry, this vulnerability that she didn't ask for and that she knew was going to come back to bite her in the ass.

Instead of reaching for him as she wanted to, she flung up defensive words. "How'd you get in here?"

A key, no doubt an exact copy of hers, dangled from his outstretched fingers. Without thinking, Elle snatched it and flung it into the corner, hoping it might land in the toilet. No such luck.

"Isn't that an abuse of power? I didn't say you could come in."

But, God, she wanted him here. She shouldn't. He'd walked out on her just hours before, leaving her broken and alone.

His eyes raked down her body and a warm buzz washed through her. After the way he'd left, she'd been so afraid she'd never get to touch him again. Relief mixed with a bone-crushing desire that made her grip the edge of the glass door for support.

"Hotel personnel have the right to enter any room we need to. It's part of the fine print you signed when you checked in."

"That's…underhanded, Officer Edwards."

"That's business, Ms. Monroe."

"Why are you here?"

"Why wouldn't I be?"

"I lied to you."

"And were planning on stealing a painting in my care."

Her lips twisted into a grimace.

"But you didn't."

"No."

He reached for her, clearly not caring that water rolled down his outstretched arm to soak the cuff of his sleeve. His fingers ghosted across her skin, flicking one of her already puckered nipples.

She'd laid all of her cards on the table, opened herself up to him and told him the truth. And he was still here.

He'd come back and, right now, she wasn't willing to look a gift horse in the mouth.

Elle wrapped her hand into the material covering his chest and tried to use the handle to pull him into the steamy shower stall.

"I'm dressed and you're wet. Why don't you come out here?"

"You have exactly thirty seconds to lose whatever you don't want ruined before I use some tricks my father taught me and have you on your knees in front of me."

"You really think you could take me?" Zane, apparently reading that she was dead serious, began hopping on one foot and then the other as he shed his shoes, socks, pants and shirt. She thought maybe, just maybe, he'd broken some sort of record considering he had at least fifteen seconds to spare.

"I think I could enjoy trying." She grinned at him, impish and excited.

"Something we both agree on."

Indrawn breath hissed through his teeth as Zane stepped into the shower. "Holy hell, that's hot."

Elle shrugged. "I like a little punishment with my pleasure."

"Either that, or the pain receptacles in your skin no longer work."

"That, too."

The heat didn't stop Zane for long. His arms snaked around her body, pulling her tight against him even as he backed her against the cold glass surrounding the shower. The sharp contrast sent a shiver through her body.

She would have thought that after her long minutes

beneath the spray, her skin would have become desensitized to heat. She'd have been wrong. Wherever he touched her, she burned. The scalding water was nothing compared to the heat of him.

His mouth latched on to her body—her neck, her shoulder, her lips and puckered breasts. He was frantic. And she loved it. Loved knowing that she could push him to that extreme with little effort. If she hadn't been so frenzied herself, she might have stopped long enough to wonder what had put him in the state. It was...unexpected.

His hands scoured her body, tweaking, rubbing, massaging and teasing. Her knees sagged beneath her, her fight to hold herself up against his onslaught lost when it'd barely begun.

Zane didn't wait for her to cling to him for support. Instead, he reached down, grasped one thigh and wrapped it high above his hip. Holding the other, he filled his palm with the globes of her rear and boosted her up until she had no choice but to wrap her other leg around him and hang on to him for dear life.

Although, she wasn't complaining.

Her back scraped over the glass. Her skin, sticky with moisture, squeaked against the cool panes.

His long, hard erection jutted between them. As his mouth was occupied lapping up the droplets of water that clung to her neck, Elle wiggled her hips in the hope of joining their bodies and ending the pressure building between her thighs.

He wouldn't cooperate.

She grasped him, positioning the head of his penis at her weeping entrance, but he refused to thrust inside. Instead, he used the pressure of his body against hers to pin her hips where he wanted them and to hold her still.

He imprisoned her hand between them, still wrapped tightly around his erection. She could feel the blood as it flowed through his veins, could count the escalating pulse of his increasing desire.

The tiny thrusts that Zane did allow did nothing more than brush the head of his cock across her already-swollen flesh. Several times, he slipped inside, pulling a gasp from her before she realized he'd go no farther than an inch.

And she wanted so much more. Knew he could give her so much more.

She whined, a sound she hadn't made since she was a child. One she wasn't exactly proud of making now. But if it got her what she so desperately wanted, it would be worth it.

"Zane," she begged as he ravaged her body and pulled responses from her she'd never experienced. Never known existed.

Lifting his head, he looked deep into her eyes and then reached for the condom he must have thrown onto the shower shelf before he'd gotten in. She was thankful he'd thought of it, because she surely hadn't.

Her head fell back against the glass and her hips seized forward when he finally gave her what she wanted. The first thrust was amazing. How could she become so addicted to the sensation of him in such a short space of time?

And there was no question, she was addicted. She needed him, wanted him, with every breath she took.

What would happen when he was gone? Would she survive the withdrawal?

Her brain fogged and her eyes glazed over. She knew they were still open, because they were focused on Zane. On his beautiful, dangerous, absorbed face. But the image was hazy, without borders.

Wedged between him and the solid surface at her back, Elle rocked her hips in time to Zane's thrusts, trying to pull every speck of delicious tension from their connection. He stroked deep inside her. Her body bowed against the building pressure until she finally exploded.

She shuddered. Her eyes slid shut and her mouth gaped open on a silent cry.

It wasn't long before he joined her. His groan of satisfaction ruffled the hair at her temple. He wrapped himself around her and held on tight. Elle understood his need to find an anchor in the storm of passion swamping them both.

She wasn't sure how long they stayed that way, melding into each other. Reality slowly set in. Ice-cold droplets pinged her face and a shiver that had nothing to do with residual pleasure snaked down her spine.

"How can you stand that?" If she was getting sprayed by cold water, he must be getting pounded.

Unwrapping her fingers from the stranglehold they'd had on his shoulders, she ran her hands down his back. His skin was freezing.

Picking his head up from where it had landed, he looked blearily into her eyes and asked, "Stand what?"

Airy laughter burst through her and she pushed against him. Reaching behind them both, she flipped the water off. Being free of his weight should have been a relief. It wasn't. She wanted to wrap her limbs back around him and never let go.

But that wasn't going to happen.

Opening the door, she grabbed a waiting towel and enveloped herself in its warmth.

"Wanna share?" Zane walked up behind her, his large hands reaching for the seam of her plush wrap.

Elle swatted at him. "Get your own." And walked into the bedroom. She'd laid some clothes out across the bed before she'd gotten into the shower. They were a glaring reminder that she had somewhere else to be tonight.

Somewhere she had to go alone.

She glanced over her shoulder as Zane walked out of the bathroom behind her, carrying a towel. The last remnants of steam escaped around his head. He was naked. Her mouth went dry at the sight of his muscular body. She wondered if the view would ever get old. Not that she'd be around long enough to find out. Droplets of water clung to the dark hair that sprawled across his chest. She felt a resurgence of desire sweep through her body.

Sex with Zane Edwards was like a drug she couldn't get enough of.

Elle bit down hard on her tongue to keep herself from saying something stupid.

When he finished drying off, his hair was standing straight on end, more wet than dry. He methodically rolled the towel into a tube before draping it around his shoulders. He grabbed the ends with both hands, evening them up. She'd bet he didn't realize he was doing it.

Turning her back on him, Elle began to drag the black shorts and simple tank over her body. She didn't get very far before Zane was making every effort to stop her. His quick fingers tugged at her zipper, trying to prevent her from pulling it up. She twisted her hips out of his reach and finished the job anyway. He snatched at her shirt, grabbing a fistful.

"What are you doing?"

"I would have thought that was obvious." She let the action of pulling her shirt over her head muffle her words. And tried to ignore the way the back of his hand brushed against her ribs when he fought her every move. "Getting dressed."

"Yeah. Why? We have all night. I need to talk to you."

She dipped and spun out of his grasp. "You have all night. I have somewhere to be. And whatever you have to say will have to wait until later. I'm going to be late." With some clothes on, she had a slightly better chance of getting him out of her room than she'd had minutes before.

"What? Where?"

"Not that it's any of your business, but I'm meeting someone."

His eyes turned a stormy, angry, sickly green that reminded her of the sky just before the only tornado she'd ever seen had ripped across her hometown.

Neither event had heralded anything good.

"Meeting someone."

She knew exactly what he was thinking. And had no intention of disabusing him of the notion that she was meeting a man. It was probably better this way. Cleaner. He wouldn't feel the need to say things he didn't mean when she left and she wouldn't feel the need to bawl hysterically like a ninny.

Win-win. All right, win-lose. But she was going to lose either way.

"Who?"

Turning her back on him, Elle rummaged around in the mess atop her dresser, ostensibly looking for a piece of jewelry. Really, she couldn't look him in the eye and lie to him. Not anymore.

"None of your business."

His hands wrapped around her body and spun her to face him. "What we just did makes it my business."

His stormy eyes sparked off her own temper. That and the fear still coiling inside her stomach like a snake eating its own tail…and her happiness with it.

"You're wrong. What we just did makes you my lover, not my keeper."

His fingers dug into her upper arms, holding her in place. The edge of the dresser bit the small of her back. And an ache started directly in the center of her chest.

"Who?" The single word was as intimidating as the expression on his face. It was quiet and deadly, just as she knew he would be when looking down the business end of a gun.

"None of your business," Elle bit out between her teeth. She was so tired of dealing with controlling men who needed to know her every move.

Ripping his hands from her body, Zane threw his arms wide. "I thought you were done keeping secrets from me, Elle. I thought you were done being evasive. Done lying."

He didn't say another word. And she didn't respond. She couldn't, not with a lump lodged in her throat.

Instead, she watched in agonizing silence as he yanked his clothes on and stalked out of the room, slamming the door behind him. The reverberation echoed through her, amplifying the already painful ache. She slid to the ground. Her back pressed against the dresser and she drew her knees tight to her chest.

Why had she ever opened that magazine?

IT HAD TAKEN HER THIRTY minutes to pull herself back together. Marcy gave her a hard look, but didn't say anything about the red tinge to her face. Instead, she'd led her into the back of the resort. Elle expected the rooms here to be less somehow. Less expensive. Less plush. More institutional. She'd been wrong.

Simon hadn't skimped on anything in the back of the house. In fact, the area felt even more like a home than the rest of the resort. Warm tones, rich woods, expensive furniture and colorful accessories greeted her everywhere.

Even the few offices that they passed had a homey feel. Family photographs, knickknacks and purposely eclectic furniture gave them that personal touch. She supposed when you lived and worked on the same island, it couldn't be helped. Work and life got tangled up when you were on call 24/7.

"Simon's the only one of the staff who lives in the main building." Elle heard the slight pause as the word *staff* tripped out of her mouth. She wondered what was behind the hesitation, but realized it was none of her business. "Everyone else either lives in private bungalows at the back of the property or in mini apartments near their job quarters."

"You mean, like the cook lives close to the kitchens?"

"Exactly."

"Sounds very…" She thought about it for a moment before the right word popped into her head. "Stressful. I love my career, but when I had a nine-to-five job, I needed those hours away from it for my sanity. Sounds like it's difficult to find distance here."

Marcy laughed and her lips twisted. "You have no idea. But there are benefits."

"Like a five-star chef at your beck and call and the Caribbean outside your front door?"

"Yeah, those."

Still, Elle could see tension tightening Marcy's shoulders as they approached Simon's quarters. She had no idea what was going on between the two of them, but whatever it was had stress whipping through the other woman. And Marcy didn't strike her as the kind of person who let stress get to her very often.

She was extremely competent. She could handle anything, in the middle of a hurricane if she had to.

Stepping off the elevator, they continued to the only door on the left side of the hallway. Marcy had barely inserted her key card before the phone at her hip chirped insistently. Lifting a finger and apologizing with her eyes, Marcy moved to the side to answer it, taking the key with her.

Elle couldn't hear any of Marcy's end of the conversation, although the way her shoulders stiffened told Elle it wasn't good.

"You have got to be kidding me," Marcy said, heading for the elevator before she'd even hung up.

She was standing inside the elevator before she remembered Elle. Whatever it was really had her in a tizzy. Slapping her hand onto the closing doors, Marcy frowned back down the hallway at her.

"I'm sorry, Elle. One of the kitchen staff cut herself. It sounds pretty bad. Our on-staff doctor's called the hospital in St. Lucia to request a rescue helicopter. We're going to have to do this later. Can you see yourself back downstairs?" The doors were already closing before Marcy was even finished talking. "I'll call your room when I'm sure she's taken care of."

The mechanical hum of the elevator dropping five

floors filled the quiet hallway. Elle's eyes were drawn to the door, the only thing separating her from the painting she'd longed to see just once more.

She was leaving tomorrow. She could get inside. Easily. She knew how to open that door. For a minute her conscience tweaked, but she immediately squashed it. There was a difference between what she was doing now and what she'd originally come here to do. She had no intention of walking out this door with the painting in her hands. All she wanted was to see it.

And she didn't think that was too much to ask.

Elle made quick work of the lock. The door shut behind her, wrapping her in darkness. It took her several seconds patting down the wall to find the light switch. Her eyes were immediately drawn to the walls. She couldn't fight the anticipation that made her hands shake.

From her memory of the photograph, she knew instantly that the painting wasn't in the front room. The only option was the last room, which would have a view of the water.

She made herself walk slowly through the suite, like a chocoholic doling out one square of Hershey's chocolate at a time. She was certain the view of the moon over the water was gorgeous, but she didn't see it. The moment she walked through the doorway into the office, her gaze landing on the painting that had meant so much to her.

A single shaft of moonlight poured across the painting, giving it an edge of mystery, as if it that were the only way it should be viewed. Considering the subject and the location of the painting, Elle could almost believe that was the truth.

She stopped three steps away, close enough to reach

out and touch the face of the woman who had meant so much to her.

Tears pricked the back of her eyes. She hadn't expected to feel this well of emotion. Nana was gone and had been for a very long time. When the painting was stolen, it was as if her grandmother had died a second time, leaving her alone again.

That loss hadn't been any easier to deal with at twenty-three than it had been at sixteen. It'd hurt.

Seeing the painting again should have brought nothing but happiness. Instead, a stab of pain shot through her chest, an echo of what she'd felt downstairs when she'd told Zane to leave.

"Oh, Nana. I've really screwed up everything, haven't I?"

She reached for the frame. She was going to have to walk away and leave the painting behind, but just for a little while she could have Nana close again.

The metal line anchoring it to the wall resisted her efforts to pull it down. Elle worried that they'd attached some sort of alarm to it. But after several seconds, something gave and the heavy canvas fell into her arms. The weight of it surprised her and had her toppling backward.

A sharp spike of pain lanced through Elle's hip as she hit the hardwood. Her legs sprawled at awkward angles beneath the straight edge of the frame. But her fingers stayed wrapped tightly around the edges, refusing to let it go.

She sat there, stunned, for several seconds. The accelerated pump of her heart thumped erratically inside her skull. Her vision began to gray and suddenly she realized she'd been holding her breath. Letting it out in a single whoosh, Elle wrapped her arms snugly around the painting and just hugged it to her body.

Relief washed through her. Unfortunately, it was short-lived.

Zane's voice cut through the peace she'd been hoping to find. "What the hell are you doing?"

Elle whipped her head around, surprise quickly crowded out by dread. She could only imagine what this looked like.

Zane's eyes blazed at her, accusing and unforgiving. "You really are a thief."

13

WELL, SHE'D COME FULL circle. Was it only five days since she'd been here before, handcuffed to a spindly chair in the middle of a closet? It sure felt longer than that.

Elle supposed a lot could happen in less than a week.

She rattled the handcuffs against the slats at her back, hoping the noise would convince Zane to actually come into the room and talk to her.

He'd been like a wounded bear ousted from his den way before spring. Growling. Snapping. Biting at her with words that cut straight to the bone. Unfortunately, his tirade meant he hadn't heard a single word she'd said.

Elle knew sooner or later this would all get resolved, but until then, her shoulders were really aching. It was like when your nose itched because your hands were covered in paint and you couldn't scratch it… She desperately felt she needed to move her arms, because she couldn't.

Suddenly she got her wish. And as she craned her

neck around to look at Zane standing in the open door-way to the closet, she wished she hadn't.

He was pissed off. No, that wasn't entirely true. Oh, he was angry, but beneath that was a layer of hurt that made her heart ache and gave her a spurt of hope she truly didn't need. Because it wouldn't make any difference.

She'd seen that same belligerent expression on her father's face more times than she could count. Zane wasn't in the mood to listen to anything she had to say. He might have stopped yelling at her, but his ears still weren't open.

He'd question every word that came out of her mouth.

It hurt that he didn't know her well enough by now to realize there had to be a perfectly good explanation.

She suddenly had plenty of anger of her own to deal with.

He shut the door behind him, closing them into the cramped room together. Desire unfurled inside her, sweet and slow. Her traitorous body could remember only the way he'd made her feel and not that he currently had her handcuffed.

Zane walked around her, leaning against a shelf that held cleaning supplies, toilet paper and enough paper towels to supply the entire resort for months.

His eyes flashed dangerously and his arms crossed over his chest. She tried not to notice how the position strained the sleeves of his T-shirt against his biceps. It wasn't exactly the right time, but apparently her libido wasn't listening.

She expected him to start asking her questions, to try to dig into her psyche. Instead, he stood there staring at her.

She didn't appreciate the silent treatment. Unwilling to wait patiently for his next onslaught, she decided to start one of her own.

"Why are you here?"

She'd surprised him, whether with her actual question or because she'd asked one at all, she wasn't sure.

"Here in this closet? I would expect that was obvious."

"No. I know why we're in this closet."

"Why is that?"

"Because you're an idiot who doesn't listen to a damn thing. I was not trying to steal that painting."

"Sure." His lips thinned and his jaw tightened.

"Why are you on this island?"

"To work."

"Bullshit. You're here to hide."

"I'm not hiding."

Elle leaned as far forward as her bound hands would let her, staring straight into his watchful gaze. "Liar," she whispered. The single quiet word had more impact than if she'd screamed it, because they both knew it was the truth.

"Why can't you trust me, Zane?"

"Because you've lied to me at every opportunity."

Her lips pulled down in a frown. She now understood how celebrities felt when their words were taken and twisted out of context.

"I haven't ever outright lied to you, Zane. I've kept things to myself, but so have you. That painting is important to me."

"I get that."

"No, I don't think you do. Nana was the one thing that kept me sane. Kept me from running away every other week. Kept me from feeling like a complete failure. Kept me from believing I was useless and had no value to contribute to the world."

"Isn't that a little melodramatic?"

"Probably. But I was a creative teenager with a bent toward emotional outbursts. I felt—still feel—everything very deeply. And the only person in my life who understood that was her."

"But that painting isn't her."

"Don't you think I know that? But it's the only thing of hers that I have. And because it's a picture of her, when I'm upset I can talk to her like I always did. She might not answer back, but she's there."

His fist slammed down onto the shelf behind him, rattling the metal and making her jump in her seat. "Do you think you're the only person who's ever lost someone important?"

Elle stared at him for several seconds, her eyes wide before compassion took over. She could see the pain now, clear as day, shining through the window of his ever-changing eyes.

"Is that what happened? Is that why you're here?"

He made a sound in the back of his throat, a cross between a growl and a whimper. "Yes."

She waited for him to elaborate. When he didn't, she asked, "Who did you lose? A partner?"

She'd seen that lost look in her brother's eyes when his first partner had died in a traffic stop gone terribly wrong. Survivor's guilt.

Zane's throat worked silently for several seconds, the muscles in his neck undulating. As he shook his head, no.

His eyes darted around the room, landing everywhere but on her. She wanted to help him. Wanted to reach out and make it easier, but experience had taught

her the hard lesson that she couldn't. She could not
shoulder the pain for this man. She could share it, if
he'd let her. But he had to allow someone inside first.
He had to admit that he couldn't have stopped the inevitable.

He had to admit that he wasn't Superman.

"My fiancée."

ZANE'S BRAIN WHIRLED. He didn't want to think about
the past, about Felicity. Not now. The past and the pres-
ent had somehow become entangled and he couldn't
figure out why.

Felicity had nothing to do with the fact that Elle had
used him, lied to him and tried to steal from him…from
Simon. He castigated himself for believing her. He'd
been ready to speak to Simon, to ask his friend and
boss to bend the rules for this woman who'd wanted
nothing more than to take from them all.

And yet, there was some correlation. He couldn't
drop the feeling that just as he'd failed Felicity, somehow he'd failed Elle. Failed to protect her from herself
and a headlong rush into trouble. Failed to give her
what she'd needed, forcing her into an action that had
unforgivable consequences.

As angry as he was with her, he was also angry with
himself. And despite not wanting to talk about the past,
somehow the words tumbled from his lips.

"I met Felicity in college. We dated for a couple of
years, but went our separate ways after graduation.
Both of us had plans and weren't in love enough to
change them."

"Yet," Elle said softly.

He was amazed how quickly she'd sized him up and

assessed the situation. A sad tug turned the edges of his lips.

"Yet," he repeated. "Later, when I moved to D.C. with the agency, I ran into her again. She was working on the hill. She'd started low and worked her way up as a speechwriter for a senator. In college, she'd been an ambitious girl with big dreams. When I saw her again, she was this sophisticated, competent, intelligent woman who'd actually conquered the world."

A restless energy buzzed through Zane's body. He wished the room were big enough so that he could pace. If he tried to pace in here, he would be walking circles around Elle, and somehow that felt terribly wrong.

"She sounds perfect."

Zane laughed as his eyes caught hers. They shared a moment of understanding that was unexpected given the circumstances. "She wasn't. Felicity was controlling. Demanding. A real pain in the ass sometimes. She tried to understand that my job required me to keep secrets, to disappear for days or weeks without word. She handled it better than some, but there were times when she just couldn't take any more."

Memories flooded Zane. Felicity throwing a vase at the wall behind him as he left late one night, shards of ceramic spraying around him. Other times she'd cried and her tears had ripped him apart. He'd broken promises, stood her up. He'd had to. The chase, the case, had always been more important than anything else. He'd always chosen the job.

"Don't misunderstand. She was a successful, independent woman."

"But even successful, independent women need the reassurance that they come first."

He nodded. "And she didn't. And knew it."

Elle frowned. "So what happened?"

"It was my fault."

"I have a hard time believing that."

Her words drew his gaze again. He stared into her eyes, trying to make her see the truth in his own. "Believe it."

Quick snatches of things he could never change and desperately wanted to forget flashed through his mind like a bad home movie.

"I had a bit of a reputation."

"As a hard-ass?"

One side of his mouth lifted.

"As a rogue agent. I was good at my job. I enjoyed the brainpower it required. I enjoyed the physical aspects. I liked that no two days were the same. But most of all, I lived for putting bad guys away. Knowing that I'd made a difference, made the world safer."

This time it was Elle's turn to laugh. "God, you're all the same. Ask my father and brothers and they'll feed you the same line of bullshit."

Crossing his arms over his chest, he raised one eyebrow. "Bullshit?" That's not what he would call it.

"Yeah. You like being in control. You like playing with guns. You like the risk and the way it reminds you that you're alive. You like the accolades and the label of hero. I don't doubt that you really do have a streak of justice that flows through your veins, but don't pretend you don't need the other parts of the job."

She had a point. "All right, I won't. The satisfaction and adrenaline are addictive."

She nodded, her eyes sharp. It was one of the things he admired about her, the way she picked up on little details everyone else seemed to miss. The way she could look straight through him and see the truth, whether he wanted her to or not.

"The point is I bent rules."

"Not you."

"Not anymore. I bent them when it was necessary. When the risk outweighed the reward of getting some asshole off the streets. One of my first cases was to collar a known terrorist. The problem was that the only allegiance he had was to money. He bounced from one dictator, one terrorist group, to another. The minute we got close, he'd disappear. I spent years chasing the guy. It became personal."

Elle nodded, an understanding he hadn't expected shining in her eyes.

"It took me eight years to get enough on the asshole to try and take him down. He was pissed off. Apparently our little dance had become personal for him as well, and he didn't take kindly to losing. Unfortunately for me, he walked on a technicality. The judge ruled some evidence I'd collected wasn't admissible because it hadn't been obtained legally."

The anger he'd felt that day blew through him, just as powerful as it had been then. Turning, he slammed his fist into the wall behind the open shelving. It was either that or roar like the wounded animal he really was. And he didn't want to lose control in front of Elle. Wouldn't let himself show her just how vulnerable this confession was making him.

"As he was leaving that day, a free man, he stopped me in the hallway of the courthouse. With this sadistic smirk on his face, he told me I'd regret the day I tried to screw him over."

Zane kept his back turned to her. Bracing his arms on the shelf, he arched his spine and rested his forehead on his folded arms. "I believed him. I'd been after the guy long enough to know he didn't make idle threats.

"I just never thought that he'd use Felicity." Zane turned to look at her over his shoulder, needing to see the expression in her eyes. "You have to believe me, if I'd thought she was in danger, I would have done… something."

"Of course you would have. I don't care who you were then, that protective streak of yours is a mile wide and I'd guess hasn't changed since you were a little boy."

Zane opened his mouth and breathed slowly through his parted lips, relief that she understood washing through him. Her opinion shouldn't matter—she was a thief after all—but it did.

The images, gruesome and unbelievable, revolved through his mind. He flinched, unable to hide the unwanted response. He closed his eyes, hoping the slideshow would stop. But it never did. Once it started, he would have to live with it for days. That was one reason he didn't talk about it.

The day she'd died, he'd raced home, finally realizing what the asshole had intended. But Zane was three steps behind instead of his usual two steps ahead. The apartment door was standing open. He heard Felicity's lone scream and tore through the apartment.

When he reached the bedroom and saw the window wide open, the gauzy white curtains fluttering in the breeze, he knew he was too late.

Something told him not to look, but he couldn't stop himself. Leaning out into the beautiful spring day, he looked down and saw her. Broken. Bloody. Lifeless.

They told him she had died on impact. But he knew

she'd been scared before then, and he hated himself for bringing that into her life. Even for a single second.

They'd given him a leave of absence, which he'd fought tooth and nail. He'd spent every waking moment tracking down the culprit, determined to make him pay.

Turning to face Elle again, he looked her square in the eyes and told her the one thing he'd never told anyone else. "I intended to kill him. I didn't care if that meant the rest of my life in jail—he was going to pay for what he did to Felicity."

"Oh, Zane." Her words were garbled, caught in the back of her throat. He was dead calm and she was fighting back tears. Somehow, that seemed appropriate.

"I never got the chance. A competitor did the job for me. Took him out with a sniper shot to the head. Did the world a favor. Did me a favor. The day I heard about his death, I resigned. I couldn't do the job anymore."

"You needed a break, Zane. You have to cut yourself some slack. You didn't push her out that window. You didn't kill her. He did. And he paid for it. Maybe not the way you wanted, but he paid."

He nodded, realizing that her words were nothing but the truth. Unfortunately, they weren't a truth he'd given himself permission to believe. Still wasn't sure he could.

She leaned forward, rattling the handcuffs against the wooden slats of the chair. He wanted to take the damn things off, but he couldn't. He knew what he'd seen, and he didn't trust his desire to believe her. His mind was clouded where she was concerned, just as it had been with Felicity's murderer. He'd been too emotionally involved, seen what he'd expected to see—an attempt on his own life—instead of what was actually staring him in the face.

"You're too good to bury yourself here, Zane. There are people out there who need you. How many drug dealers, terrorists, murderers and rapists have you taken off the streets? How many lives have you saved? How many more could you save? You don't belong here, Zane, and you know it. Deep down inside, you know it."

He took a single breath, pulling oxygen deep into his lungs. Shutting off every emotion that was swirling unchecked through his body, Zane turned his gaze to hers and stared deep.

"You're wrong. This is exactly where I belong. No one else will get hurt as long as I'm here, in the middle of nowhere."

"Jesus, you're stubborn." She threw herself back in her chair, her body slumping against the waiting cradle of the bars.

He opened his mouth to say more, but was cut off as Simon burst into the room, followed quickly by Marcy.

"What is going on?" The exasperation in Simon's voice was palpable. "I thought we'd already worked this out. What is she doing back in handcuffs?"

Zane sagged against the wall between two shelves, his anger and zeal having spun themselves out during his confession.

"I caught her stealing a painting from your office."

"The one you told me was stolen?"

Marcy pushed past Simon to stand before Elle. "Why would you do that, Elle? I thought you only wanted to see it. I believed you."

Elle stared up at the other woman. "I did only want to see it. I wasn't trying to steal it. After you left, I was standing in that hallway and all I could think was that I was so close and I just knew my final chance to see

Nana again was slipping away. I'm leaving tomorrow. I couldn't wait."

She turned her gaze to Zane's. "I was taking it down to get a better look, to touch her face, and the hanger snagged on the nail. I fell on the floor when it gave. I had every intention of putting it back and walking out of that room. Without the painting."

Zane's mind spun, like wheels stuck in mud. He wanted desperately to believe her. Too desperately. Was the innocence he saw in her eyes real or show?

But one tiny phrase stuck in his mind. "Marcy." He turned to look at the other woman. "You were with her?"

"Yes." She nodded. "I was taking Elle up to see the painting when I got an emergency call and had to leave." The other woman's eyes swung to Elle's. "I said I'd call you later. Why didn't you just wait?"

Tears gathered at the edge of Elle's lashes, turning her gray eyes a sparkling silver that he couldn't look at. Damn, why was this so hard?

"I've waited for four years, Marcy. I couldn't wait another minute, not when I knew she was so close."

"Wait. Elle, that painting is yours? It was stolen from you?" Simon moved farther into the room so he could look at her.

The space wasn't big enough for all of them. The air suddenly felt thick and cloying.

Elle looked at Simon. "Yes. The picture is of my grandmother. It was stolen from me four years ago. I thought I'd lost it forever until I saw it in that magazine."

"I knew that photo shoot would be nothing but trouble." His light sarcasm might not be appropriate, but it was typical Simon. "Why didn't you contact me?"

"I did. You ignored all my letters, emails and never returned my phone calls. I assumed you knew it was stolen and didn't want to deal with me. I consulted my lawyer and I had about a zero chance of getting it back through legal channels. I can't prove that it's mine. It was a gift to my grandmother and my father gave it to me when she died—no will."

Simon raked his fingers through his hair, a scowl tightening his face.

"Zane, how much did I pay for the damn thing?"

He'd studied the single piece of paper that had come with the painting, a bill of sale. Had it memorized.

"Seven thousand, three hundred and twenty-five dollars."

"Is that all?"

Zane nodded and waited to see what his boss would do.

He turned to Elle and shocked them all. "For God's sake, take the damn thing. I don't have any attachment to it. I spend that much on clothes every month."

Zane knew that was a lie, but he wasn't about to throw his friend under the bus at the moment.

Elle couldn't hold back the tears that had been threatening. They began to flow silently down her cheeks. But her voice was crystal clear when she asked, "Are you sure? I'll pay you. I don't mind paying for it."

"The hell you will. It's yours and you shouldn't have to pay for something that already belongs to you."

"But you bought the painting in good faith."

Zane cleared his throat, but Simon beat him to the punch. "I didn't bother to ask for evidence that the painting was clean. That's my fault. Buyer beware. Trust me, I won't make that mistake again."

This time it was Marcy's turn to snort her disbelief.

Simon flashed her a look that was both a warning and an acknowledgment that she was probably right.

Simon pointed his finger at Zane and said, "Unlock these handcuffs." Then he turned to Marcy and continued, "Have the painting packed and ready to go in the morning."

He turned back to Elle. "You are still planning on leaving in the morning, correct?"

Elle nodded her head, happy to do whatever he asked.

"Great. Now that my evening on the mainland has been ruined, I'm going to lock myself in my office. Unless the place is on fire—" his glaring gaze swept each of them, including everyone in the threat he was about to make "—really on fire, no one better disturb me until at least noon." He was halfway out the door before he revised his statement. "Better make that two."

Marcy turned on her heel and followed him out, but not before Zane noticed the way her shoulders tightened with annoyance.

Neither one of them bothered to close the door behind them. Zane crossed the room slowly, trying not to let the still-drying tracks on Elle's cheeks affect him any more than they already had.

He reached behind her, working the key until the cuffs popped open.

She pulled her wrists into her lap, rubbing the red bands that circled them both.

After several seconds she looked up into his face and asked, "What happens now?"

The hope in her eyes mocked him. His chest tightened. He didn't want to watch her leave.

But he couldn't ask her to stay.

He couldn't risk giving her that kind of power over him. Over his happiness and his sanity.

Losing Felicity had been devastating. Something told him that if he let her, Elle could become even more important to him. Losing her would hurt that much worse. And she was so reckless....

He couldn't go through losing someone he cared about. Not again.

14

"What do you mean? You'll leave on the morning ferry, with the painting that you came for."

His words arrowed straight into her chest. She fought against the urge to curl her body protectively over the wound that only she could see.

"That's it? It was nice to know you? Thanks for the great lay? Don't let the door hit you in the ass on the way out?"

He walked away from her again, depriving her of seeing his face. Just as well. It was blank when he turned back to her, and she didn't think she could have watched that mask slam down. Not after he'd just opened up and shared the most devastating moment of his life with her.

"What do you want me to say, Elle? That sex with you was amazing? The best? True. That you make my blood boil with lust and frustration? Absolutely. That we don't have a future? I think you already know that. We've known each other for less than a week."

"Sometimes that's all you need."

"That's all you need. My guess is you fall in and out of love three times a week."

Elle sucked in a breath as if he'd actually punched her instead of wounding with words. It would be easy to fold in on herself and give up. But that wouldn't be true to who she was and she refused to let this devastation he was handing out affect her that way.

Instead, she went with anger. "First of all, I never said I was in love with you." Thought it, but never said it. "Second, that's a lousy thing to say and I don't think you actually believe it. I think you want to. It's easy to convince yourself that, because I go off half-cocked, tend toward emotional outbursts and make myself vulnerable that I don't know what I want."

She stood, trying to ignore the pain that shot down her spine from the awkward position she'd been in for hours.

"You're wrong. I know exactly what I feel. And, yes, I'm in love with you." Okay, now she'd said it. Hadn't really intended to, but that didn't mean the words weren't true.

He scoffed, the sound scraping against her nerves. "How can you know that, Elle? You barely know me. And for most of the past week neither of us even liked each other."

"That's not true. I always liked you. I just didn't like that you were following me and keeping me from doing what I'd planned."

"You mean, I kept you from committing a felony."

She crossed her arms over her chest, trying to protect herself from the truth of his words and what was happening. "Maybe."

Throwing his hands up, Zane cried, "We don't have a future. You live in Atlanta. I live here. You're just starting to build a name for yourself as an artist. Do you think you could keep those important contacts going if you moved to a tropical island? I have a job."

"That you hate."

"That I don't hate. I'm not willing to uproot my life for something that probably won't last through the end of the summer."

She walked slowly toward him, dropping her arms and her defenses. She'd always been the kind of woman to fight for what she wanted, and only heaven knew why, but she wanted Zane in her life. She shouldn't. He was the type of man she'd always avoided, sworn she'd never let in.

But as Nana had often told her, with that sparkle in her eyes and a smile tightening her wrinkled skin, you don't always get to choose who you fall in love with.

Elle pressed her body against him. She didn't reach for him. She didn't pull him to her. She didn't kiss him. Instead, she stood on tiptoe so that her body rubbed against his and let the zing of electricity fly between them.

And did the only thing she could think of that might jolt him in to taking a chance. "Coward," she whispered against his lips.

His entire body stiffened beneath her, but she ignored it. "You're afraid to feel again. You're afraid to let your heart thaw enough to let someone else in. You can't let go of the guilt and forgive yourself."

She looked up into his eyes, waited until she had his full attention and she knew he'd hear her words. "It was not your fault."

He pulled his gaze away and, in that moment, she knew she couldn't win. Nothing she said would change his mind. Stubborn man.

A lump formed in the middle of her throat. She swallowed it down. Finally pressing her lips to his, she let every ounce of her love and passion and hope and happiness bleed into their connection. For several seconds, she lost herself, in the hope that the kiss was real and that it would do what her words hadn't.

But he didn't wrap his arms around her or pull her into his body. Instead, he stayed still, his white-knuckled fists the only proof of the effort it had taken him to not respond. She took a step backward. And then another. And another. Until she was at the door.

And he just watched her walk away.

"YOU FRICKING IDIOT." Marcy's words held no heat, but Zane felt them all the way down to the soles of his feet.

He'd been avoiding her for the past week, a little difficult considering they worked on an isolated island. Every time she'd walked into a room, Zane had walked out. Until now, that strategy had worked, but he'd known it wouldn't work forever.

However, avoiding her had given him something else to concentrate on. Something other than missing Elle with a fierceness that bordered on obsessive.

He wondered what she was doing. Who she was with. If she'd finished that painting of the waterfall.

If she was safe or had gotten herself into another one of her scrapes.

He'd bet his salary on trouble.

Unfortunately, he couldn't escape from Marcy this time. She'd managed to corner him in his own home. She currently stood inside, hands on her hips, exasperation blazing from her eyes.

"When are you going to go after her?"

"I'm not." Resigned to his fate, Zane plopped onto his bed, the only seating in the place.

"Then you're even more idiotic than I thought. Zane, you're in love with the woman. Go after her."

"And tell her what? That I can't stop thinking about screwing her?"

She smacked her forehead. "Men. Do not lead with that. How about telling her that you miss her and want her in your life."

"Why would she agree to that?"

"Because she's as much in love with you as you are with her."

"I'm not sure that's enough."

Sadness crossed Marcy's face as she walked across the room and sank onto the bed next to him. "That's terrible."

"I only met her two weeks ago."

"What difference does that make?"

He shrugged. His heart told him it didn't matter. But his brain kept yelling at him to run hard and fast, to avoid anything that could bring him to his knees the way Felicity's death had.

"You're scared."

It wasn't a question, so Zane decided not to answer. That didn't make it untrue. Elle's last word echoed through his head. *Coward.*

"No one could blame you, Zane. You went through hell when Felicity died."

"I never told you about her."

"Simon did. Do you think he'd hire you without telling me everything?"

No, probably not, although Zane hadn't really thought about it before now. "You can't protect everyone—including yourself—from everything, Zane.

Didn't your job teach you that bad things happen to good people? All we can do is make the most of whatever time we're given. You have to take a risk. Take the risk or get out of the game."

"I thought that's what I was doing."

Marcy shook her head. "Poorly. You've been walking around this place like a wounded bear for the last week. I'm starting to get complaints. Zane, you don't belong here and we both know that."

Two weeks ago he would have argued with her. But something had changed.

"Neither do you."

Marcy's pert nose wrinkled at his words. "We're not talking about me right now."

"Yeah, yeah." If he was honest with himself, he hadn't enjoyed being on Île du Coeur for months. At first he'd needed the solitude and the undemanding job so that he could heal. And while he wasn't sure he would ever completely conquer the guilt, at least he'd been able to admit that Elle was right. He wasn't the one who'd pushed Felicity out that window.

Marcy reached over and placed her hand over his. "If you don't take this risk and start living again, Zane, then you might as well have jumped out that window after her."

A lump formed in the back of his throat. Zane forced it down. Damn it, he hated when Marcy was right.

"Who knows? It may turn to shit. But at least you'll have put yourself back out there. It's time to stop hiding and start building a life again."

Elle's words, almost identical to Marcy's, had been haunting him for days.

"Marcy, I hate to do this to you."

"But you quit. Yeah, I know. Good thing I've been calling around for your replacement."

Tugging at her ponytail, he said, "Minx."

"It's a good thing you came to your senses or I was going to have to confiscate some sedative from the infirmary and ship you to Atlanta. Your replacement arrives on the afternoon ferry."

This time when he tugged, he pulled a little harder.

"Ouch," she said, grabbing at her scalp. "You have three hours to pack." Marcy looked around. "Shouldn't be difficult. Looks like you never actually unpacked."

No, he really hadn't. The island had never been home. But then, for a very long time he hadn't known where he belonged.

Maybe he'd finally figured it out.

15

ELLE SAT IN HER STUDIO, staring at the blank canvas in front of her. She'd been doing the same thing for the past four weeks.

Well, that wasn't entirely true. The first week, she'd moped around and been too upset to think about working. The second and third weeks every time she'd picked up a brush Zane had managed to make his way into the painting—no matter what the subject was. Hell, she'd even tried her hand at something abstract, a style she hadn't used since art school. And still, she could see his form in the random lines and splattered dots.

This week, she'd decided not to try painting at all, to give herself some time away.

But that hadn't helped. She'd gone shopping in the little farmers' market downtown and nearly had heart palpitations when she thought she saw Zane in the crowd. She'd even gone to visit her father, hoping a plunge back into her rigid childhood home would remind her why she and Zane wouldn't have worked out anyway.

It was one thing to maintain a fling for a week, it was entirely another to build a relationship that could last.

Someone should explain that to her heart.

Instead of the reminder she'd needed, she'd ended up crying on her father's shoulder—something neither of them really liked.

But he'd been there for her, in his gruff and stiff way, telling her that any man who didn't realize how special she was was a moron. She'd needed to hear the words, even if, as her father, he was obligated to say them.

And so here she was, staring at the canvas, itching to load paint onto the brush and just let go. And scared to let herself do it in case she would regret the picture that would form before her.

Although, she probably shouldn't be. In the past few weeks she'd done her best work, fueled by the emotions jumbled inside her.

Taking a deep breath, Elle closed her eyes and let herself go. With vivid, sure strokes, she layered paint onto the canvas. She had no idea how long she sat there. Hours definitely. She ignored the growl of her stomach and quenched her thirst with her trusty bottle of water only when she took two seconds to step back and stare.

Zane's face, in profile, took up most of the canvas. Stern, determined, with that slight tilt to his lips that hinted at more beneath the surface he showed the world. In the lower right corner, she'd put herself. Staring after him as he walked away.

The yearning on the face of the girl, who was her yet somehow wasn't, made her stomach clench with re-membered dread. Sadness shadowed her eyes and ten-sion filled the straight lines of her body.

Elle stared at it for several minutes, trying to objec-tively evaluate something she was entirely too close to.

But after a little while, a light dawned in her head. It was her grandmother's painting in reverse.

Instead of the beginnings of a fledgling love affair, it was the end of an unrequited love. Instead of highlighting physical passion, it demonstrated emotional devastation.

And maybe it would finally give her closure so that she could put the event behind her…. And maybe it wouldn't.

Arching her back in a valiant effort to work out the kinks, Elle decided that, either way, she needed a break. Besides, according to the bug-eyed cat clock on her wall, her oldest brother would be here soon.

After the incident with her father, the men in her life had circled the wagons and begun taking turns checking on her. At first, she'd balked at the suicide watch, trying to convince them that she truly was okay. At least, okay enough not to need daily surveillance.

They hadn't listened. It had taken her a few days to realize they wanted to be there for her. With her. To make sure she knew there were people in her life that did care.

It was really sweet. But it was also getting old.

Tromping into the kitchen, she stopped long enough to wash the splattered paint from her hands, before fixing herself a quick sandwich.

She hadn't realized just how hungry she was—one sandwich was definitely not going to do it. She was rummaging in the back of her fridge, trying to find something that wasn't either out of date, insanely unnutritional or completely unappetizing, when a loud knock sounded on her front door.

Not willing to leave the hunt, Elle yelled out, "Come on in, Bobby. It's open."

With a grunt of unhappiness, she pulled out an apple that didn't look completely wizened. As soon as Bobby left, she'd grab her favorite pecan chicken salad from the deli around the corner.

Apple in hand, she started backing out of the fridge.

"Who the hell is Bobby?"

Elle smacked her head on the top shelf of the fridge. Swore. Slapped her hand onto the crown of her head in the hopes of holding her throbbing brain inside her skull. Spun around.

"Holy hell." It was all she could say. Zane Edwards was standing in the middle of her kitchen.

She looked awful.

She had on her nasty, paint-splattered overalls. Her hair was pulled to the top of her head in a messy ponytail that she'd absently run her fingers through, making it even messier. She'd bet there were streaks of paint all the way through it. She probably looked like a deranged clown.

"Not exactly the reception I was hoping for."

And then the anger surfaced and saved her from herself. "Just what were you hoping for, Officer Edwards? That I'd knock you to the ground, tear off your clothes and pick up where we left off?"

His eyes began to glitter, with mirth and a desire she really didn't want to see right now. His lips twitched, but at least the man had enough sense not to actually let them smile. "Well, I wouldn't have minded that."

"Too bad. That isn't going to happen."

"A guy can dream, can't he?"

"Not you. Not about me."

He took a step closer to her, and Elle fought the urge to take a giant step back. She didn't want to show him weakness, to let him know he could still affect her. But she also didn't trust herself. If he touched her, she might actually start ripping his clothes off and drop him to the floor.

"Elle." The single word was a warning, but she wasn't sure about what. Every muscle in her body tightened, thanks to the fight-or-flight response rushing through her system.

"I just want to talk."

"About what? You made it perfectly clear we had nothing to discuss. You made up your mind."

"Can't I change it?"

"No, that's a woman's prerogative."

Hope was blossoming inside her chest, a hope she didn't want. A hope she didn't trust.

He took another step forward, his voice dropping. "I'm sorry I hurt you." The words melted down her spine, seductive in their own right without the added benefit of his raspy, sexy voice. He'd done that on purpose, the bastard. Used his bedroom voice to utter the apology she didn't want to hear, yet wanted desperately.

She speared him with her eyes, looking straight into him and letting him see every ounce of the pain he'd caused her.

"You broke my heart."

His throat worked for several seconds. She watched the smooth, tanned column as his Adam's apple bobbed. It was easier than looking into his eyes and seeing pity there. She didn't want that.

"Excuse me for not being as quick on the draw as you are. I'm not as…emotional."

"An excuse."

"All right, I'm a coward. Is that what you want to hear? I was a coward."

Elle couldn't help herself, she lifted her gaze and

looked into his green eyes. The golden flecks and deep brown swirls mesmerized her. She wanted to look away but couldn't. She wanted to hate him but didn't.

"I'm an idiot, Elle. Fortunately for us, that isn't a crime. I didn't realize how important you'd become to me until you were gone. I didn't believe I could come to love anyone as quickly as I fell for you." A gasp caught somewhere in the back of her throat. Did he just say what she thought he said?

"In fact, I didn't think I'd ever love anyone again."

The pain in his eyes sent an answering stab through her. She didn't want to see him upset. She didn't want him reliving that nightmare again.

"You don't have to do this Zane."

"You deserve the words, to know what I feel for you is different from what I had with Felicity."

Elle shook her head, trying to understand what he was saying. "What do you mean?"

"I mean, you've ruined me for other women, Giselle Monroe. I can't even look at another woman without comparing her to you. Your open smile. That feisty set of your jaw when you're about to do something stupid and brave. The way you fight for what you believe in, not willing to take *no* for an answer."

"I took *no* from you."

"Only because I didn't give you a choice. And trust me, I'm not going to give you one now. I quit my job. I've already found a place to rent here in Atlanta. I'll find work as a security consultant or I'll go back to school and maybe get another degree. I'll sit outside your apartment every night until you let me in. I'll follow you on every date so that I can ruin it."

"You're going to stalk me?"

A smile tugged at the corner of his lips, but she could see the determination in his eyes. He wasn't kidding.

"If that's what it takes."

"Good thing I'm such a pushover."

"Does that mean I won't have to commit a crime?"

"I don't know about that," she drawled. "I have this thing for bad boys…"

She let out a squeal when he reached for her, lifting her high in the air before crushing her back down against his body. His lips found hers, devouring her in the kind of kiss that made her knees give out.

"You're not getting an apartment. I want you right here where I can keep an eye on you," she managed to whisper before he pulled them under again.

Both of them jumped when the crack of her door slamming against the wall echoed through the apartment.

Before she could react, Zane pushed her behind him and stood in front of her as a human shield. He really had to stop doing that.

"What the hell is going on? Giselle, I heard you screaming."

Her brother came into the apartment, swinging. The words weren't even out of his mouth before the first punch collided with Zane's jaw. If Zane's hands hadn't been firmly on her hips, holding her behind him, he probably would have defended himself. As it was, he refused to let go of her long enough to fight.

It turned out she was the one who came to his rescue.

"Bobby," she yelled. "Stop that right now."

Pushing Zane's hands away, she slid in between the two men. They both towered over her, glaring at each other. Zane tried to yank her back behind him, but she resisted. Bobby wrapped a hand around her arm and tried to move her, too.

She didn't appreciate being treated like a chew toy caught between two junkyard dogs. But at least neither of them could take another swing with her between them.

"Bobby, this is Zane. Zane, this is my oldest brother, Bobby."

"This is the asshole who made you cry?" her brother asked, while simultaneously trying to reach over her and clock Zane again.

She pushed at his chest and landed a swift kick to his shin for good measure.

Bobby hopped on one foot, doubling over to grab his shin with the other.

"What did you do that for?"

"To keep you from doing something stupid. Zane's staying, so you might as well figure out how to get along."

"What do you mean, he's staying? I thought you never wanted to see him again. Let me throw him out for you, Ellie."

Elle turned her back on her brother, smiling across at the man who held her heart in his hand.

"Nope, he's staying." She grinned as Zane warily shuffled his gaze between her and her brother. "And as penance for your bad hospitality, you're going to talk to the chief and see if he needs a consultant on staff."

"A consultant for what?"

Elle grasped Zane's hand and pulled him up beside her. "Meet Special Agent Zane Edwards, recently with the CIA."

"CIA," her brother parroted back, scowling at Zane with distrust.

She had little time to worry about her brother's prejudice against anything federal. Not when she was dizzy from Zane spinning her to face him. His arm snaked around her waist and he pulled her close once more.

It was electric, and possibly illegal, the way her body responded to him.

"Do you know, I think that's the first time you've actually used my real title?"

"That's because I like being able to brag. Before I was trying to push your buttons, now I'll take anything I can use to keep you right here with me. Even if that means getting you a job with the APD, so my dad and brothers can keep an eye on you."

His lips drifted down to hers, but at the last second he stopped them from actually touching, casting a wary glance at her brother. "I'd rather *you* keep an eye on me."

"Oh, don't worry, I have every intention of doing that, too. Besides, I think it's your turn to wear the handcuffs."

With a growl, Zane crushed his lips to hers.

And somewhere in the back of her mind, she heard her brother say, "Elle," in that exasperated way of his before he slammed out the door.

Epilogue

THEY STOOD TOGETHER IN THE empty gallery, hand in hand. Soft light streamed down over the paintings that hung on the white walls. The blank backdrop was perfect for the colorful exhibit of Giselle Monroe originals.

Zane squeezed her hand. "Are you happy?"

She laughed. Only Zane would ask her that question right now.

"Well, I sold every last painting tonight, so yeah, you could say I'm happy."

"Almost every painting."

Elle twisted in his hold, bringing their bodies flush against each other. Standing on tiptoe, she whispered against his lips, "Almost every one."

She'd given him the painting she'd been working on the day he barged into her apartment—complete with paperwork that proved he was now the proud owner.

The gallery had agreed to hang it, with the portrait of her grandmother beside it, at the entrance to the exhibit. It was the perfect introduction to the showing she'd created—the evolution of their love story.

Zane had been in Atlanta for six months. He'd moved into her apartment and they'd immediately begun talking about getting a bigger place. It was perfect for one, but cramped for two. Especially with her studio taking up so much space.

He'd taken a job with a local security firm, working as a consultant to businesses in the area. The chief had asked him to work with the force, but Zane had turned down the offer. He didn't want to put her in any kind of danger. And, honestly, she couldn't protest, since his current job was safer for him, too. It offered him a way to use his skills without putting his life on the line. She'd promised him she could live with the fear—she'd done it all of her life she could do it again. But Zane had refused.

Everything was perfect.

Or so she thought, until he pushed away from her.

His expression was weird and her heart began to pound in her chest. Something was wrong. She could see it in his shuttered expression. It appeared sometimes, when he was thinking about the past and dealing with the emotional fallout that he still struggled with.

She tried to reach for him, but he moved out of her grasp. "Zane, you're making me nervous."

He laughed, a broken sound that did nothing to settle her nerves. "That's *my* job."

"To be nervous? I don't understand."

He dropped to the ground at her feet and she started to sink down beside him, thinking something was really wrong, when he squeezed her hands and stopped her.

"Elle, the past six months have been the best of my life. I've been happy. You've made me happy. And I didn't think that would ever happen again."

And in the single moment, she realized what he was doing.

"Ohmygod."

His lips twitched upward before turning serious again. "I know I haven't always done or said the right thing."

"Could have fooled me. Last night sure felt right."

"Would you shut up and let me do this?"

Elle threw her head back and laughed. Tears gathered beneath her eyelashes and the biggest, brightest smile she'd ever felt stretched her face and tugged deep at her heart.

"Well, then hurry up. I want to get to the good part."

He looked up at her, his eyes shining with the love and passion that they'd found with each other.

"Whatever comes after yes. Yes, I will marry you. Yes, I will have your children. Yes, I will love you for the rest of my life. Yes, I will let you handcuff me anytime you want."

"God, you can't do anything the traditional way, can you?" He rose from his knee, pulling a small velvet box from the pocket of his sports coat.

"Nope, and you wouldn't have it any other way." Throwing her arms around him, she buried her face into his neck and simply inhaled. Her lips found the warm skin beneath the dress shirt he'd worn just for her. Her tongue darted out so she could taste the speeding pulse that meant they were both alive.

His breath fluttered the tendrils of her hair against her temple as he whispered into her ear, "Giselle Monroe, will you marry me?"

Pulling back, she looked into his eyes and said, "You better believe it."

Behind them, her grandmother's eyes watched as they embraced and Elle could have sworn they flashed for just a second. No doubt, a trick of the light. But sharing this moment with the woman who had brought them together just felt right. She'd gone to Île du Coeur looking for the past, but instead had found her future—the man holding her. She was finally happy, as her Nana always told her she would be.

*****

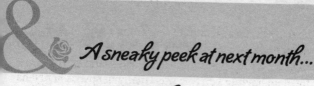

A sneaky peek at next month...

Blaze®

SCORCHING HOT, SEXY READS

My wish list for next month's titles...

In stores from 18th May 2012:

❑ Want Me – Jo Leigh

& Night After Night... – Kathy Lyons

❑ Rub It In – Kira Sinclair

& Just One Kiss – Isabel Sharpe

Available at WHSmith, Tesco, Asda, Eason, Amazon and Apple

Just can't wait?

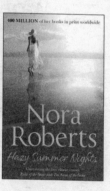

MILLS & BOON Book Club

2 Free Books!

Get your free books now at
www.millsandboon.co.uk/freebookoffer

---

fill in the form below and post it back to us

E MILLS & BOON® BOOK CLUB™—HERE'S HOW IT WORKS: Accepting your books places you under no obligation to buy anything. You may keep the books return the despatch note marked 'Cancel'. If we do not hear from you, about a nth later we'll send you 4 brand-new stories from the Blaze® series, including a -1 book priced at £5.49 and two single books priced at £3.49* each. There is extra charge for post and packaging. You may cancel at any time, otherwise we send you 4 stories a month which you may purchase or return to us—the choice ours. *Terms and prices subject to change without notice. Offer valid in UK only. plicants must be 18 or over. Offer expires 31st July 2012. **For full terms and aditions, please go to www.millsandboon.co.uk/freebookoffer**

s/Miss/Ms/Mr (please circle)
_____

st Name
_____

rname
_____

dress
_____

_____ Postcode

nail
_____

nd this completed page to: Mills & Boon Book Club, Free Book fer, FREEPOST NAT 10298, Richmond, Surrey, TW9 1BR

Find out more at
www.millsandboon.co.uk/freebookoffer

Visit us Online

0112/K2XEA/REV